SPLATTER

REAWAKENING THE SPLATTERPUNK REVOLUTION

LANDS

READ ORDER

234	8	80	182
100 (14)	114	214	
	132	26	
	148	52	
	166	246	

SPLATTER

REAWAKENING THE SPLATTERPUNK REVOLUTION

LANDS

COLLECTED AND EDITED BY
ANTHONY RIVERA AND SHARON LAWSON

 GREY MATTER PRESS

SPLATTERLANDS: ISBN 978-1-940658-10-0
First Grey Matter Press Trade Paperback Edition - September 2013

Anthology Copyright © 2013 Grey Matter Press
Design Copyright © 2013 Grey Matter Press
All rights reserved

Grey Matter Press
greymatterpress.com

Grey Matter Press on Facebook
facebook.com/greymatterpress.com

TO ALL THE ORIGINAL SPLATTERPUNKS.
THANK YOU FOR CHANGING EVERYTHING.

TABLE OF CONTENTS

HEIRLOOM
MICHAEL LAIMO

Lucienne cast heavy eyes over the man's naked body. Smiled. "You know what I've always wanted to do?"

Grunting, she reached under the dinette table into the worn canvas duffle bag, pulled out the rifle and laid it between them.

To Lucienne, its power was definite. It commanded mankind.

She grinned, saliva in the corners of her readied lips. "For so long I've wanted to..." she whispered. The man leaned forward, in agony, in ecstasy, desperate to unearth her deciding words.

But her sentence hung open, like the mystery of something wet in the shadows. She turned her back to him, did not reveal anything. Yet.

Instead she ripped a long strip of duct tape and pasted it over his hungry, bruised eyes.

Gripping the weapon, she aimed it at him, a smile ever so bittersweet.

* * *

The rifle was ancient, an heirloom passed down from grand-father to father, and then from father to Lucienne. A memento from her governed childhood, one sleek, shiny barrel running eighteen inches, the grip serrated rubber, its bulk eight pounds of steel-grey manhood able to accommodate two spiral-cased bullets: deadly ovum in a hardened shell. Lucienne would sit like a doll and watch Father remove it from the worn canvas pouch it slept in. He would clean it, smoothing the oil upon its hard surface, her thoughts re-maining somber, confused eyes following the graceful sway of his hairy fingers as they flittered about the barrel and stock, the aroma of cloth and oil hollowly contrasting her father's masculinity.

"You can look, but you can't touch," Father used to say, gently stroking the rifle with his woolly, withered hands. Her eight-year-old mind grasped the truth in his voice when he said this, the strik-ingly long rod itself a cold-hardened symbol of death—yet still, an image of Father's staunch virility.

Mother, if she had been alive, she would have frowned upon him, nodding and arguing that Father's rifle was an entity to keep a distance from, a force never to be reckoned with no matter what the circumstances. "Wisdom governs the female mind," mother once said. "Brawn, the man's."

Lucienne nodded at the time, her silence an affirmation of her understanding and her knowing that she would never forget.

"Someday, my precious," Father would say, "this will be yours."

* * *

Lucienne had been too young at the time to understand mother's untimely death; she hadn't even known exactly what death was. She was only five at the time, and who explains to five-year-olds about death and dying anyway? She'd heard some of the folks in the hospital mention the word *stroke*, but Father always used the term *go away*. Whichever, she wondered how long it would take for mother to be done with her death and come back to her so she could ask questions about the food she ate and the clothes she wore. Father would have nothing to do with those things.

A few people had gathered in her home a day or two after mother *went away*, all of them sitting quietly in the small living room and sipping wine. Father had pulled Lucienne aside, asking her if she wanted to say goodbye to mother. She looked around at the bowed heads of those in attendance for some guidance. No one coached her into making a decision, so she simply nodded.

Father picked her up and carried her down the humid hall into the bedroom where Lucienne had never really been allowed to go. Her eyes caught full sight of the ceramic and glass figurines that mother kept on the dresser, the ones that Lucienne could never ever touch even if she asked nicely. Father once told her that when mother went away, she would be allowed to touch anything she wanted, even if other people said it wasn't okay. Even mother's figurines.

Strangely, Lucienne felt pleased that mother had gone away. It seemed that Father was too.

You can touch anything you want...

A large, shiny box sat in the area where the bed had been. In it lay mother, looking different than she usually did, so pale and still, wearing her lacy, pink evening gown and patent leather shoes, her make-up done extra-special. Lucienne felt a rush of blood bullet-ing through her body, an odd, fearful zeal that seeped through her chest, and then her stomach, and finally into the spot between her legs. This thing she was looking at was *death*. *This* is what all the pale-faced, wine-sipping grown-ups were talking about. They weren't talking about mother, they were talking about *death*.

No wonder they did, Lucienne thought. *It feels so good.*

She remembered how good it felt at that moment, to be in Father's arms, staring down at mother, at *death*, and then at Father's hairy hand—the same hand than ran the length of the gun barrel as it cleaned the surface—as it massaged the spot between his own legs.

Yes, death feels good for all.

She returned her gaze to mother, contemplating her flat and sunken eyes. Her cheeks, dulled gray and wrinkled, the dry, delicate fibers breaking through the weathered cracks of her lip-stick. It felt so good to be there at that moment, peering upon her detachment from the world, Father there to reassure her that someday, if Lucienne listened, she would return from her death to be with her again.

Lucienne listened.

But mother never returned.

The pleasures returned and culminated when Father cleaned his gun. He'd disappear into the woods behind the house for the entire day, Lucienne left home alone to tend the household neces-sities, mopping the floors, doing the laundry and making sure that the workbench had been adequately prepped for cleaning: a crisp sheet, cool pillows, perhaps a blanket on cold nights. Father would bring home an animal of some sort, a deer, raccoon, a pheasant, the skins stripped away to reveal the inner beings.

Father would carve the meat from the animal's bones, the sickly-sweet smell of viscera and gristle invading her nostrils in bursts.

Then afterwards, Father would sit on the sheet Lucienne laid out next to the workbench and clean away the gunpowder staining the rim of the rifle's shaft, smoothing the oil up and down and up and down as thick, biting fumes rose up and commingled with Father's rich musk.

You can look, but you can't touch...

In due time he would slip the rifle away, its canvas casing swallowing it whole, and as he did would press his thick, meaty hands against the jeans he wore in that feel-good spot between his legs. Lucienne would sit through his slow routine, truly enjoying the bulging image of the gun beneath its casing as it divulged its ultimate secret to her—an intimate purpose that only *she* could taste and understand. Father would stare at her, then remove his jeans and lube himself with gun oil, and she would watch with great intrigue as his brow beaded, sweat pouring from his pores, his grin growing tighter and tighter at the corners of his mouth, his jaws bouncing up and down in gross ecstasy.

And Lucienne's mind would wander over the secrets the rifle revealed to her, of the killing stories, each and every tale a breach of solidity and persistence, a means of gathering dominance. Lucienne could find the capacity within herself to follow Father's lead, to take into her hands the power and finesse that Father displayed to her all those years.

You can look, but you can't touch...

Father would shudder one last great time and then hastily fire his own shot, his bullet softer, more yielding than those inside the rifle. But no less deadly.

Years passed before Lucienne finally found the strength within her to make the demanding decision to bow down to her calling. She'd made every attempt to act accordingly, continually agreeable in answering to Father's call. She felt obliged to him; after all, he did feed her and provide shelter for her. And, he never really did *touch* her. But as the years pressed on and she grew towards adolescence, so did her anger, blooming within her body, mind and soul like a flourishing cancer, spreading its poison through her blood until it finally erupted, its concentration boiling at the foundation of her heart, tainting her previous focus of well-meaning and goodness with something black and hideous. She could feel it. She could *taste* it. A complete transition, her life newly guided and influenced through venom and anger.

She had heard the gun calling to her from its place in Father's closet. Sleep had eluded her one night when Father cleaned his gun twice, and she followed its whispered beckoning into his room— the room she hadn't been permitted access—quietly crawling on all fours into the closet as he slept, carefully lifting the gun from its canvas nest. It felt truly wondrous, grander than the warm images of the gun oil slathering the slender barrel in any cleaning session. Heavy was its bulk in her pre-teen hands, hands that hadn't had the experience of touching much in her life.

You can look, but you can't touch...

Here she had her first orgasm. An amazing pleasure, pounding through her body like crashing thunder in the mountains, utterly restful and flushing, her hands shaking so uncontrollably that she dropped the gun.

It went off.

The bullet ripped through the deadened silence, the mattress at once sending a storm of feathered stuffing airborne like a blast of snow, white as they went up, red as they floated down. A burst like a flower appeared on the wall behind the headboard, bits of Father's skull and brain adding texture to the wicked design now permanently etched into her brain.

She could feel herself breathing. Its cadence ran a rhythm with the surge between her legs. Nothing had ever felt so fucking good.

Shaking, she took the gun, the casing, the bullets, and fled into night, never to return, her mind at once conjuring the things she wanted to do with the rest of her life, knowing that everything she accomplished would be spurred solely to arouse passion, to create pleasure.

Father had said, "Someday this will be yours."

Today was that day.

* * *

The rifle had become her only companion, its cool, lengthy shaft her only lover, its casing her blanket of security. Her environment had shifted from the backwoods of the country to the inventive streets of the city, the hustle and bustle of a million accents brushing by her, keeping their safe distance if she invaded their personal space. Lucienne lived her life in fear, she, still a virgin for all intents and purposes, the world around her ready and willing to rape her for the very meat on her bones.

She dreamed of Father nightly and everything he'd taught her, and she hopelessly desired returning to a day where she could realize his distant touch again. But was that possible? Perhaps. Physically, he had never laid a sweaty trigger finger on her. Yet still, he'd graced her with a pleasure that no other had ever equaled, a pleasure not precisely physical, but rather mental, fattened of strength and power that magically translated into something licentious. Now, in her early twenties, these explicit desires swelled to a pinnacle, forcing the need to create her very own ecstasy. A personal paradise not much unlike the Eden Father had secured all those years.

I could do it, for now, I can touch...

She gazed at her naked self in the mirror, at her alabaster skin, at her facial features, remotely European, at her waifish body, the hipbones slightly protruding, the bottom ribs visible beneath the swell of her miniscule breasts. She applied her make-up, circling her eyes with black liner, burying her full lips in deep red, setting purple-red pancakes into her cheeks like angry bruises. She filled all her piercings, eighteen in all: one in her tongue, one in each nipple, two in her navel, two in her left eyebrow, one in her lip, one in her clitoris, nine at various places in her ears. She squeezed herself into a patent leather dress, her ass cheeks resembling two black teardrops, her breasts pushed up and out so the very edges of her nipples were exposed. Standing tall on spiked heels, she adjusted the dress so her strapless shoulders were straight; her naked back stiff and proper, appropriately exposing the angular tattoo on her shoulder blade. Finally done, she stared at her tall, svelte body and tried to determine if her pain—her desire—would show to the outside world, if her bruise-colored eyes truly weighed down on her appearance like two open wounds.

There weren't any visible scars. But her pain was observable, tangible.

Good.

Before escaping into the night, she retrieved the gun from beneath the bed and gently removed it from the casing.

She placed her blood-red lips to the tip of the smooth barrel, kissed it gently.

Smiling, she left to begin the hunt.

* * *

The place she chose catered to the black-shrouded clientele with whom she'd become familiar, those people whose androgyny equally matched their sexual preferences. It didn't matter what sex you were as long as you were willing to express yourself freely and comfortably, not too passively, not too dominatingly.

The night passed in common themes, sweaty prayers of ritualistic sex, the dance floor an orgy of reaching limbs groping the nearest flesh, exposed or not. Sweaty torsos writhing to the incessant thrum of techno beats, minds lost in the fervor of sustained moments.

Lucienne weaved through the club, her body in constant motion, not in dance, but in subtle pursuit of prey. She kept her methodology unobtrusive, her image inconspicuous, never allowing herself to be noticed lingering in one place by any one individual for any lengthy period of time. She continued on in this unassuming manner, head bobbing ever so slightly to the beat of the music, her legs taking short, self-assured steps, her back softly maneuvering the graceful sway of her shoulders. She was the hunter, she was *dominant*.

Her eyes finally locked onto the perfect target: a man, six-foot, middle-aged, not necessarily a true component of the surrounding lifestyle, but rather an individual seeking escapism from the hideously routine world. A broker perhaps, maybe a lawyer, or a businessman. Someone seeking to be hunted down for one night, to be made. He had a beard and moustache. Slightly overweight, a tired bulge squeezing over his belt.

He looked just like Father.

It had been months since the last one like this, an obvious target alone at the bar, unmoving except for beady eyes that searched the human mesh for a lover. She knew, he was the one. She had to have him.

His eyes locked with Lucienne's.

She smiled kindly, feeling wet.

Then approached him.

* * *

They stood outside the door of her apartment, the man's eyes perusing the fourth-floor landing, his distorted features a testament that his common sense fell in clear conflict with his fleshly desires to press on into the adventure of the night. In the pallid light—dull but running much brighter than the chaotic darkness of the club—the man didn't really look that much like Father after all, and in that sense appeared to carry the possibility of threat. His forehead was much too furrowed, his eyes too round, his beard a bit too neat. But still, there was something about him, a sort of strange sadness surrounded him; the same pathetic glee that had blanketed her father's hungry image when unwanted and uncontrollable desires beset him.

They went inside.

She instructed him to sit on the bed, his rotund body jiggling as the thin mattress sagged beneath his weight. She moved to the only table in the apartment, a small dinette, and sat at one of two chairs, two fingers exploring her wetness along the way, knowing and relishing all over again that she—like Father—had become a hunter, hungry and reckless, her cause pure defense from the enemy-past that had perpetuated her persecution.

That still continued to tempt her.

When she looked up from her reverie the man was naked, a harsh coating of hair and moles riddling his husky gut. He smiled, teeth yellowed from years of morning coffees and cigarettes.

He stood up, smiling evilly.

Beneath the table, Lucienne slipped the rifle from its pouch.

He marched over to her, and when he reached the opposite side of the table she showed him the gun. His eyes winced, his face blanched, cheeks trembling in sudden panic.

"Sit down," she instructed, and he obeyed. Tears clouded his eyes like a rushing tide. "You know what I've always wanted to do?" she asked.

"What is this?" the man asked, his grin showing a brew of fear and strange excitement.

Still holding the gun she pulled a strip of duct tape from a roll on the floor alongside the gun casing and squeezed it over his eyes. He protested, albeit slightly. She ripped another strip and placed it over his mouth. Gooseflesh rippled his skin, the coarse hairs on his neck and arms standing on end.

Good. He was enjoying himself.

He mumbled something through the seal on his mouth, Lucienne answering him by pressing the barrel of the gun into the left side of his groin, just below the base of his penis, just above the scrotum. His penis hardened, his balls turned purple. Her body trembled with a rush of warmth, her nipples stiffening beneath the hot material of her dress.

"Hmph!" yelled the man, voicing his pleasure.

"Shut up!" Lucienne barked the words in the harshest tone she could induce. Using her free arm she plunged an elbow into his face, bruising the cheek purple. He tumbled off the chair and landed on the hard floor with a dull thud, his erection nearly tearing on impact. The sour tang of sweat rose into Lucienne's nose, an odor signifying to her the progression of lustful respect.

Perhaps he *was* the perfect target after all.

She pressed the rifle into the small of his back, running it down the trail of gooey sweat leading into the fissure of his ass, the cold metal leaving red streaks pressed into his flesh. Placing the spike of her heel into the center of his back, she brought the gun up and placed it in her mouth, tasting his salt, tempting her taste buds, the cool twang of metal blossoming upon her tongue as she traced it about the shaft, flitting in and out of the hole. The man kept his sightless gaze to the wood floor, now stroking his purple erection and moaning incoherently.

Pulling the gun from her mouth, she quietly placed it upon the table. She then yanked the man up by the hair. Dragging him along, she pushed him to the bed, face down.

"Stay," she chided.

She retrieved the gun and utilized it to force his legs apart, exposing his anus. Curiously, she stared at the mahogany circle, its coarse hairs forested in crust, chunky dimples pocking the land-scape of flesh surrounding it.

She hiked her dress up over her head, exposing her nakedness only to the mirror hanging on the wall over the headboard, aptly angled so that she could see herself and her current prey on the bed, his face wincing behind the duct tape. She tightened her grasp on the gun, blowing out a long, clogged breath. The man waited, breathing heavily through his nose, a tensed hand on his penis.

"Up on all fours," Lucienne demanded.

The man obeyed, shifting clumsily, his fat dangling obscenely. She prodded his great, white ass with the end of the rifle, taking a poke here and there at his swinging testicles. The man moaned, in pain, pleasure, whatever.

She kneeled on the bed next to him, gripping his thigh for support, then flicked her tongue along the crack of his ass, deep into his anus, pressing the gun ever so closely to her lips. She alternated, swallowing the barrel of the gun, then lubing the man's dark, sour membrane, back and forth and back and forth, wholly participating in an ungodly ménage à trois. Tiring easily, she backed away, slapping the man hard on his buttocks. "Don't move."

She reached under the bed and grabbed the container of gun oil, twisted the top and squeezed a healthy dose of the shit-colored liquid onto the barrel. It glistened as she lubed it up, her hand sliding up and down and up and down.

Just like Father used to do.

Kneeling a foot or so behind the man, she tenderly prodded the crack of his ass, leaving puke-streaks of gun oil on the shore of his flesh, greasing the surrounding hairs until she eventually ferreted out his soft hole. She took a deep breath, felt an orgasm nearing, then buried eight inches of the oily metal barrel inside him. He grunted, stroking his penis fervently.

Lucienne's life played back in her memory, her father and his hunting trips, her mother whose life Father had undoubtedly extinguished in order to carry out his profound desires. A lethal combination giving birth to her own sick desires, the gun at its crux, her approaching orgasm its only aspiration.

The man gripped the edges of the bed, the sheets bunched in his grasp. By now the gun oil was burning the tender walls of his anus, but she showed no mercy, pounding furiously, eyes closed in prayer for orgasm, one gentle finger instinctively searching out the trigger. The man began to howl behind his gag, tried to pull away. Lucienne plundered forward, going deeper, her orgasm teasing her, but not giving in. She wanted it to last forever, her dripping flesh spraying upon his, staining the mattress, the prevailing smells of gun oil and musk and shit in the hot room.

She continued to pound. The man thumped in a panic, tried to wrestle away. But never enough to fully disconnect himself from the harsh encounter. Lucienne went deeper, both hands on the gun. Blood started pouring from the man's ass, streaking the barrel. His skin went from white to deep crimson.

His body stiffened.

And then the man came, his seed oozing from his urethra to the mattress in a weak globule.

He collapsed, ass in the air, permitting Lucienne to finish, to achieve her ecstasy.

She continued to pound her fury, unable to stop until she experienced the only love she knew. The gun slid in and out. Her muscles tensed, her flesh rippled. She felt her eyes roll up in her head. *Yes!* It came, an orgasm of proportions unfathomable, her muscles tightening up in great trembling quakes, sending electrical shudders throughout her body, from her head to her heart to her toes.

And, to her fingers. They tensed, contracted...squeezed.

The explosion was muffled, felt more than heard. At the same shuddering moment her vagina sprayed its orgasmic juices, the man's body jerked forward in a deadened heap, an alarming spray of red blanketing the clear droppings of semen on the bed, splashing her naked body in a great river of release. The gun fell from her grip, and it slipped free from his anus, now devoid of contraction. She collapsed back, exhausted, clearing her face of the man's splattered gristle.

She stayed silent for a few moments, admiring tonight's effort as her urges waned. Just like the animals Father used to bring in from the woodland, her prey lay steaming on her bed, glistening entrails torn free from their cavity, slick blood pumping from various fissures. The putrid smell of death rising in swells. Gouts of blood and bile spilling from his mouth.

Another night, another successful hunt, the bullet unheard.

She rose from the bed and went to the kitchen. Removed the knife from the sink. The one with the twelve-inch blade. She placed it on the scarred dinette table.

Before skinning her prey, she would need to perform a task: clean her gun. Father's gun. Grandfather's gun.

She would enjoy every scintillating moment of the process, just as she did when she was a child, all those years ago.

ABOUT THE AUTHOR
MICHAEL LAIMO

Michael Laimo has published seven novels and three short story collections, previously in paperback with Leisure Books, and now available in e-book from Crossroad Press. Two of his novels have been nominated for the Bram Stoker Award: *Atmosphere* (First Novel category) and *Deep in the Darkness* (Novel category).

Laimo's novels *Dead Souls* and *Deep in the Darkness* have been made into feature films for NBC's Chiller network.

His work has been published in six languages, and he continues to produce short fiction for markets in the United States and in Italy.

VIOLENCE FOR FUN AND PROFIT
GREGORY L. NORRIS

Wrapping your mind around the fact that most people deserve to die is the hardest part. But once you do? Murder, well, that part's fairly fucking easy.

* * *

Her name was Penelope. I bashed her head in—and you'll love this detail—with the old doorknob. You know that term *gray matter*? They got it wrong, I tell you. Once you split through a skull or crack open a face, the glop that oozes out is orange—like a Dreamsicle. And red from all the blood. Those fiery, beautiful, basic colors were the only thing remotely pretty about her. Penelope needed to be taken out. Deserved to die. Bear in mind, a doorknob alone isn't the most effective weapon, but when you screw it into the head of a baseball bat, well...

She took quite a few more whacks to fell than I anticipated, and I'll admit the last dozen or so were probably unnecessary. She lived in a gated community. There were cameras all over the place. Too bad for her there wasn't one in the trunk of the bitch's Benz. You learn a lot of skills from reading books—like how to pop a trunk, how to liquidate the enemy, how to take from them what they stole from you.

I walked out of Penelope's house with over ten thousand in cash and a lot more in jewelry, which I pawned in Vegas. The guy barely glanced at my mustache, just handed over my ID and the money so I could gamble more in the casino next door, because they love it when you play loose and fast at the slots. Love it when you pawn the family jewels and engage the Devil.

Not sure how much the Devil really had to do with my little trip to California. There are at least a million people out there who think the person who liquidated the CEO of Wide Country Mortgage Specialists—"America's Number One Home Lender" and a key player in the mortgage crisis that led to economic disaster and tent cities filled with homeless across the nation—should be beatified as a modern saint.

* * *

Who am I?

I am no one. I am everyone. I am shadow. I am light. I am somebody who has read a great many books. When you're homeless, living in a small niche hidden behind the cement stairs of your local town library, you spend your days savoring the warmth inside the building, reading to pass the hours, the *weeks*, urinating and bathing in the public head, stealing coffee out of the staff lounge after you've mentally absorbed the routine enough so that you can sneak in and out unseen.

As for the nights? You huddle behind the stairs, listening to the occasional footsteps, growing angrier and more bitter at the realization that you're being walked over, stepped upon, by so many rotten souls. And one day you just snap, knowing you're going to get even. You're going to take your revenge in blood. You're going to kill.

Never do you imagine how good you'll be at it. Even more curious, how much you'll love it. *Love* it so much, you wonder if you'll do it for sport, even if they hadn't backed you into this dark and desolate corner.

* * *

It doesn't require much in terms of financial investment to take out another human being. People have been clubbing the fuck out of one another for fun and profit dating back to the cave. When one considers the availability of cliffs convenient for shoving an adversary over, all those rocks just lying about, simply perfect for crushing heads, and branches that can be swung like clubs or sharpened into spears and pikes, not to mention the plethora of natural toxic substances so easily slipped into the slop people shovel into their mouths... It's a wonder that primitive man ever made it out of the Dark Ages alive.

What my first official kill lacked in theatrics more than made up for in the end result. You see, I would lie awake, too terrified to sleep, feeling the cold in my aching joints, my sex, my bones. I went from being in my mid-twenties to the century mark throughout the course of that first transformative winter.

I was never a material person. I only wanted the givens that any other relatively benign, sane human aspires for: a warm home, a hearty meal, and if not the true joy that comes from seeing one's dreams realized, at least an illusion of moderate happiness.

To have those basics, I took a job in a hospital, helping people. Noble, yes, I know—I was so naïve once upon that other time. But I truly went into this position as an orderly in a busy emergency room thinking I might like to take courses to become a nurse. Foolishly, I told the woman that hired me that I also loved to write, that I was tinkering with a novel, had published several short stories in the pretentious rag of my local community college. That I was hoping to buy my own house. A little house, nothing special or spectacular. This was at the height of the real estate craze when the predatory lenders were giving away loans to cats and dogs.

She was a fat cat, figuratively in regard to her finances—for the hospital and her crooked union made sure she was well off—and also in the physical sense. Her ass had four cheeks instead of the natural two. Numerous times, as my situation degenerated, I imagined shoving explosives down the back of her massive corduroy slacks and blowing that giant sofa of an ass's cushions apart. Or shimmying a shotgun up into that place where the sun never shined, pulling the trigger, and buckwheating the bitch.

In the end, her demise was far quieter, but no less effective.

* * *

Condemned to nights beneath the stairs, I would dream of killing her. Ransacking her house for anything valuable the way she had, after a fashion, robbed me of my precious few belongings.

This is how it went down:

I bought my little house, started taking nursing courses, but soon discovered that I was in the wrong line of work for someone who quickly grew to hate people. Oh yes, *hate*, though I hadn't hated people at the onset. Being scratched and spit at, coughed and shit upon by the patients you're trying to help has a way of turning a person's opinion toward the dark end of the spectrum.

I came down with the flu. Two months later, pneumonia. Pneumonia led to bronchitis. Bronchitis degenerated to asthma. In six months, I racked up more sick time than during the full scope of my life before, even factoring in measles and the chicken pox as a kid. Sofa-ass came down hard on me and, ironically, I was suspended without pay for a week, a bizarre punishment for having missed so many shifts. I had a doctor's note—from one of the doctors in our very own ER. Clearly, I'd gotten sick on the job. It's not like, during my free time, I went in search of getting punched by drunken stragglers on Friday nights or hacked upon by ignorant twats with pneumonia who couldn't bother to cover their ugly mouths.

I know why she really fired me. Because instead of taking cigarette breaks outside the ambulance bay with the rest of the chain smokers, I sat in the staff lounge and wrote words in my journal. See, I had something other than the job which, though unspoken, was *verboten*. The job was Sofa-ass's only life. She was condemned to it. I was an outsider, always would be. A square peg among some seriously round holes. One in particular quite round.

"One more sick day over the course of the next six months and your services will be terminated," she said from the other side of her desk in the filthy shithole she called an office, a room where her sweaty odor flourished. She was armed with a manila folder filled with paper files and had print-outs on the desk in front of her. The bitch was a slave to technology, but when it came to serving up hurt, she loved a paper trail and still resorted to the old classics like official complaint forms and incident reports in triplicate.

"Fine," I said, containing my outrage.

"Sign this."

I signed it without looking it over clearly. The termination agreement, she failed to tell me, also involved any and all incidents regarding arriving late for my shift.

A month later, I walked out of the house to find my car had a flat tire. I paid for a taxi, entered through the staff entrance, and was quickly escorted back out.

I applied for unemployment. The big-assed cunt fought me in arbitration and won, claiming I was a lousy worker, a lazy one at that. With no money coming in and an adjustable mortgage rate, I lost the house. The car died. I've often thought about that flat tire and wondered if she somehow had a hand in it, thus setting in motion all that followed.

Homeless, with nowhere to go. I refused to contact any of my distant relatives for a handout. They might have offered it, but would have gloated over my misery. And so I slipped through the cracks, into an underground realm of soup kitchens, free clinics and shadow-steeped hidey-holes.

I took up residence under the library stairs and struggled to breathe, terrified but also stripped of the last chromosome of so-called civilized life. My asthma got so bad during one of the nights, I ceased breathing. In effect, I died. But then I gasped myself back from the abyss, and never struggled for air after that.

And through the frigid weeks that felt like months, I plotted my revenge.

* * *

I cut my hair, donned a knit ski cap and grew a mustache, of sorts. Under all the layers of clothes, even I didn't recognize me.

The area where the nurses smoked was around the corner from the ambulance bay. There were security cameras, sure—one of them aimed right down on the smokers. I knew the lay of the land well because I'd worked there, aware of details, patterns, and schedules, including that black-hearted cunt's daily routine.

I picked up an old umbrella at the local Goodwill store, where I'd also purchased most of my new wardrobe. But beneath the library steps where I lived in the cold—in the miserable cold—I augmented it. The umbrella was black. I detailed cheery yellow stripes on it with tape so it couldn't be connected to me. I also worked on replacing the flimsy, hollow handle with something far more solid.

On yet another cold night, I tromped to the hospital, aware of the time—so aware—and of her familiar schedule. A row of junipers lined the street. The ambulance bay sat empty, but the parking lot looked moderately full, which was great for my purposes, because it meant the smokers wouldn't come streaming out in twos or threes but one at a time. I simply needed the right one. I waited in the bushes.

And right on schedule, the bitch lumbered out, pocket book

slung over her shoulder. She fished out her smokes, lit up and sucked more poison into her ugly, toxic core.

For the first time in a very long time, I smiled.

I abandoned my cover and marched toward the ambulance bay. It was after dark, but I knew I'd be seen by a number of cameras, though not by the only one that mattered, however, because as I passed underneath, I reached up and, using the umbrella's curled handle, hooked the wire feeding images to the security guards and tugged. The camera flipped up and out of alignment.

"Hey, you," the bitch said.

I yanked on the handle, gave it a turn, and drew my upgrade down and out of the hollow core. A tire iron. The punishment, I reasoned, should fit the crime, a modus I would soon come to rely upon.

She stood with cigarette clutched between her sausage fingers, the sulfurous stink of ashtrays and brimstone clinging to her. One good, hard whack that any major league baseball player would have appreciated dropped the bitch. It also elicited the most musical note of extreme pain I had ever heard a person utter, even after working for almost two years in the busy metropolitan ER mere yards distant from the scene of her liquidation. She shrieked an aria as she fell. Blood spouted. I struck her again and again, until the crunch of breaking skull and popping eyes shuddered up the tire iron and through my marrow.

"Judge, jury, and executioner," I said. "Payback's a real bitch, *bitch*."

But she was beyond hearing me. I resisted the urge to spit—why risk giving the cops free evidence after this slain demon's body was found?

Found soon, no doubt.

I reattached the two parts of the umbrella with surprising calmness and walked away, past the bushes where I'd hid—after rifling through the bitch's purse, where I lifted a few hundred dollars in twenties. I could have gotten a warm room for the night, a hot meal. I didn't, because I was already feeling warm and giddy on the inside.

After disposing of the outer coat, the mustache, my gloves and the umbrella in a place where the police would never find them—and if they did, my disguises would be corrupted of anything traceable—I settled down in my hovel beneath the stairs and relived the details of the attack, the divine retribution that had culminated with her caved-in head.

Damn, I loved every second of it.

* * *

I don't know how good a writer I would have made. I never really got the chance. But being a killer? Well, it turns out I was good at something after all. Better than good. I was fucking *great*.

According to what I read at the library following the bitch's demise, the police were looking for someone they believed to have been a patient. Good luck with that, I thought with justifiable pride. Up the hill from the library, I'd dumped all the evidence down the sewers through a loose manhole that I'd worked open precisely for the occasion.

I could have ended my endeavors there. She was dead, the rancid whore, and I had gotten away with the perfect crime. I was invisible, nonexistent. I could have stopped, but I didn't, because

Fat-Fuck wasn't alone in wronging me. There were other guilty assholes scattered around the globe.

And so I set out to bring them all to justice.

* * *

One hears things in this new America, this broken new economy shattered mostly by greedy Republican fucks. The Dems aren't without blood or sin for helping to ruin the planet. Corporations and petty, tin dictators have risen up across the land through power grabs, wherever one turns.

It didn't take long before a second opportunity presented itself. Her name was Rebekkah. I met her at one of the soup kitchens. You could very clearly see by her demeanor that she was a lady. But her husband had beaten her to a pulp and cast her down into the mud with the rest of the lowlifes. We struck up a conversation over bowls of gruel. I listened intently, with genuine compassion and interest.

"I swear, if I could get away with it," she said.

"It's always the spouse they come looking for, so you can't. But I can."

"Huh?"

"How much is it worth to you?"

"To do what?"

"To go home. To read the prick's obituary. And to walk away, free and clear."

She said she had money tucked aside, a secret stash of cash that couldn't be traced and that her husband didn't know about. Only it was in their house, which she dared not return to. Not yet. The money was mine if I somehow grew the balls to pull it off.

"Oh, I will."

"I'm not sure..."

"Make up your mind."

"Okay, do it."

"Once this is set in motion, it can't be stopped."

Rebekkah nodded. "Don't screw it up."

"Oh, babe, I'm not the one that you should worry about screwing things up," I said with a chuckle. "Keep your head on straight and do as I tell you, when I tell you, because if you don't, the body count will be two instead of one. And I'll get away with it, because I don't exist. I'm a ghost."

* * *

His name was Axel. A real he-man's name, for a real he-man sort of guy. Fresh-faced, All-American, he loved football and fast cars and, apparently, beating up women.

Their house was one town away. I wore boots two sizes too big, the toes stuffed with newspaper and scrunched-up shopping bags, and got out of the taxi four blocks from the front door. By the time the ride was through, I'd sold the driver—a young, Hispanic dude who spoke broken English and didn't once look at me directly—on a story about visiting a sick sister and promised I'd call for a ride home to the city just as soon as I had tucked her in full of chicken soup.

I slipped along the sidewalks and through bushes, dressed in a different coat, a different winter cap. Rebekkah had told me certain details about the house. Big, new place, with an alarm system and cameras on the front yard. And a dog door.

They didn't have the dog anymore—Axel made her get rid of him. I scaled the backyard fence and scooted through the dog door into the mostly dark house. The alarm system controls were in the kitchen, which contained about an acre of black granite and stainless steel appliances.

I donned soft, disposable shoe covers I'd picked up at the hardware store and crept through the kitchen and down the hallway, toward the living room where a widescreen TV blazed. A shape sprawled across the overstuffed sofa, a head with its back toward me, dark hair in a neat athlete's cut. A handsome bastard, Rebekkah had told me, though bastard trumped handsome. I trumped both of them with one swing of the cast iron frying pan I pulled out of the same lower cabinet where Rebekkah told me I'd find an envelope loaded with cash, hidden in a lobster pot.

Lucky for her, she was right.

Unlucky for him, she was right.

The first whack didn't kill him, or even knock him out. However, when Axel went flying up and then back down, there were half a dozen empty soldiers on the coffee table in front of him. Beer bottles scattered and shattered. Axel howled out a blue streak of expletives on the way down, dug his socked feet into the carpet, and tried to stand.

"Who the fuck are you?" he roared.

"I'm no one. Oh, and your wife sent me."

I slugged him again, right across the jaw, which cracked on impact and sent pieces of bone through skin and tossed teeth like dice across the expensive hardwood floor. Excitement and arousal flared, turning my blood into high-octane fuel. Axel fell. She was correct about him being handsome. The handsomest, with his dark hair, blue eyes and swarthy, unshaven face. His five o'clock shadow after seven at night lent him the illusion of a pirate.

"Argh, matey," I said, delivering one last thunder crack to his head.

Axel didn't get up again. He also wasn't nearly so attractive after the last round.

I scattered cheap perfume from the Everything a Dollar Store and robbed his wallet—another hundred and twenty in addition to the two grand I took from the lobster pot. I then took all of Rebekkah's jewels from upstairs. The police questioned Rebekkah, who had been at a book reading at the big chain in town, her alibi ironclad, complete with author's signature, but I'd made it look like a crime of passion turned foul. 'The Hooker Homicide,' it came to be known after Rebekkah was cleared of the crime; after telling the police about the years of infidelity and abuse at the hands of a man whose hands routinely wandered across the flesh of countless other women.

* * *

In a trailer park not far away, a single mom with two kids faced persecution and eviction at the hands of the park's Nazi manager, Trish Ferber. I learned of the situation after taking on several clients through a very tightly connected and trustworthy grapevine and decided a bit of charity work was in order. Pro bono bludgeoning, if you will.

Trish—*Trash* as I came to refer to her—was a real piece of work. A piece of shit, actually. The first time I saw her standing at the trailer park's bus stop, screaming at parents arriving in cars to pick up their kids, ordering them to form a line only on the right side of the road, I knew she was a petty tyrant of the worst order. Queen of a hopeless realm and loving that she ruled over the lost souls condemned to be her neighbors; a real She-Satan cunt of the lowest variety. I'd have killed her even if I hadn't heard the tale, if for no other reason than to elevate the planet's collective IQ and class level. If I lived in North Korea, I'd have rid the world of Ding-Dong-Ill and his ilk by now. If fate had seen fit to put me in a pillowcase with a slit at the eyes in Iran, Mister Ass Mini-junk would be a memory. I was born here, in America, however, with plenty of garbage to dispose of. Like Trashy Trish Ferber.

Trash lived in a single-wide on the hill. On the day I showed up at her front door, dressed in my usual well-thought-out costumery—flannel shirt, jeans, work boots in this case, faux mustache back in place, hair under baseball cap—I knew how much fun I was going to have.

Taking out scum always makes me tingle. I've never harmed animals, never been overly fascinated with fire except for its warming properties on cold nights. I don't follow your typical psych profile for a serial killer, because I'm *not* typical. I may be the first person outside the Ukraine or the Yucatan to have turned murder into a profitable and, yes, noble business. But I do get a certain sexual tingle from time to time as a result of purifying the world of evil assholes.

The car I drove that day was new, shiny. I had plenty of money in my wallet, and when the conniving devil-snatch answered her front door, I made sure that a bunch of C-notes showed clearly from the top of my chest pocket. Dressed in a gray wife-beater that had started out white and riding jodhpurs, she eyed me warily from behind thick glasses, her gaze quickly zeroing in on the money.

"Help you?" she asked. Christ, even her voice sickened me.

"Yes, I believe you can. I understand you're the one I need to speak to about renting a *trawler* here."

"I have something that's gonna come on the market soon, sure. I'll need you to fill out an application. Come on in."

She turned. I followed her inside and surveyed the place. There were bald eagles everywhere, in artwork on walls, prints with patriotic themes, ugly ceramic ones, even throw pillows covered with the ridiculous motif. The furniture was cheap, the kind from China bought in chain department stores and assembled at home. The most garish thing was the linoleum nailed onto the kitchen countertop. The place stunk of cigarette smoke and feet. I wanted to gag.

"The available unit wouldn't happen to be 10 Adams Avenue, would it?"

"Why, yes," she said. She had a yellow sheet in hand. Her beady, rodent eyes rolled suspiciously toward me. "How did you know?"

I reached into my shirt and pulled out the cleaver. She made a play for her cell phone. I swung and chopped off the bitch's hand, right at the wrist, loving the elegant crack of the bones as the blade sliced through them. She screamed a deafening peal I hadn't thought possible from a body her size.

"Bitch," I said, and swung again, hacking her ugly head off her shoulders in one deft swipe. A fountain of blood sprayed up from the stump of her neck. The head flew over the countertop, while the rest of the bloodied mess spilled across the filthy carpets, its remaining hand scrambling for a face no longer there.

The urge to spit on Trashy Trish possessed me in a way I hadn't experienced since my first kill. I wasn't sure why I felt this job so personally. Trashy Ferber was dozens of decapitations and meted justices since.

I swallowed down the loogey before it could launch and fed half of her head into the trash disposal after chopping it into quarters. Again, every punishment should fit the crime, and as trailer trash goes, this bitch was among the worse. My last act on that particular job was to leave ten grand in a manila envelope inside the screen door at 10 Adams Avenue. I knocked, spun around and drove away. Ditched the gloves, the car, the clothes and the cleaver. Sewers made great disposal sites for my new line of work.

It dawned on me later the same night, huddled in my place deep beneath the library stairs, as to why I'd enjoyed killing that disgusting woman. I'd taken out almost everyone who'd ever wronged me—and quite a few who'd done terrible evil against others. But I'd never gone to the very source to make those who'd cost me my home pay for their actions.

Home. This was my home now. Even with so much money, so many resources, I still lived behind the stairs. I barely remembered that other place, that former me.

But I remembered quite clearly the name of the woman who'd foreclosed upon my house. The next day, on one of the library computers I booked a ticket to Los Angeles and took the act on the road.

* * *

A doorknob used in the committing of a murder is the kind of detail the police are sure to remember. Yes, it's true that I returned to my old house late one night and removed the knob from the front door. The locks were changed by the bank long before, but the house had sat empty since my eviction—one of millions owned by lenders who'd foreclosed on people whose only crimes were losing jobs and falling behind on their mortgages, thus forced to become homeless in the richest and greediest country on Earth.

I concocted a plan and mailed the doorknob in advance to a hotel in L.A., where it would be waiting for me upon my arrival. I booked a room under one of my aliases, but never checked in. I did, however, pick up my package at the front desk. Then I bought a baseball bat and other assorted necessities in a shop on Hollywood Boulevard.

I showed up at the offices of Wide Country Mortgage Specialists, where they'd already adopted numerous security measures against an increasingly hostile American public. None of their avarices were going to stop me. You see, I knew the lazy bitch would park close to the building. She'd have a vanity plate, something appropriate to her ego. Penelope's read: *Pretty Penny.*

The parking lot sat under the scrutiny of numerous security cameras. But if it's one thing September 11, 2001 showed us, rent-a-cops don't always pay sharp attention to the important details.

I parked my new acquisition, an expensive car I'd helped myself to in Hollywood, popped the bitch's trunk in short time with a cloned keyless and climbed in. Had she opened the trunk two hours later, I would have liquidated her there, on the spot. She didn't, so I rode the distance back to her gated palace. Marie Antoinette got it quickly. Not so, this little, self-proclaimed queen. I had the doorknob. I bought the baseball bat, along with a power drill, and the result was a mace-like marvel that rivaled the best of warrior weapons of old.

"Why?" she screamed.

I chased her through the house and let her know why, somewhere between the first swing and the one that busted open her head.

* * *

Here's the funny thing:

I am a master at disguise, and did a pretty decent job mastering that of the late Penelope. En route to Vegas, I texted the two other people of significance in the Wide Country hierarchy who were also instrumental in the madness of the mortgage crisis, Vice President Victor Cairo and CFO Paula Dillingham. They were already under investigation by the federal government and named by the White House as persons of interest after the talking heads were ultimately out-talked by hoards of pissed-off villagers armed with torches and pitchforks who'd lost their homes in the mortgage crisis.

I texted Cairo and Dillingham on Pretty Penny's phone: *Off to Vegas on a short road trip. Carry on in my absence. Be in touch.*

I figured that would buy me some time. After cleaning up financially in Vegas, I got another bold idea and decided to put it to use. It would be my crowning achievement, my ultimate revenge, and my gift to the people. *Vive la révolution!*

On the return trip, I texted them again: *Meet me at the private airfield. Important information for you both. This could be the thing that kills us all!*

Not a lie, so much as a bending of the truth. I'd never tackled two at a time. I'd never done anything so audacious, so danger-ous, so public. I made the rendezvous time for later that night. The Wide Country Learjet was parked at a private terminal north of LA. I got there easily on Pretty Penny's ID and attitude. Fifteen thousand in cash to the security guard at the terminal and a threat to terminate his employment did the rest.

"Ma'am, I have a mortgage," he said.

"I know—and as long as you do what I say, I won't take your home away. Here, for your trouble."

He took the money. By the time Cairo and Dillingham drove up, he'd have done the deed himself, there and then. But I wanted them to suffer for the evil they'd committed.

* * *

Wine was already poured—and laced with the Oxy I'd lifted from the bitch's medicine cabinet, crushed up and well-disguised, of course.

As they boarded the jet, I excused myself to the bathroom.

"What's the meaning of this, Penelope?" Cairo barked.

"Have a drink while I visit the Little Felon's Room," I called over my shoulder. "Trust me, you're going to need it."

I knew there'd be no cameras in this jet. The last thing these Wide Country cunts wanted was for anyone to see or record their dirty dealings. The seats, I was certain, crawled with crusty DNA.

And probably more than a few drops of dried blood. This wasn't a corporate Learjet; it was a military bomber. The bombs it dropped upon the civilian populace weren't thermonuclear or hydrogen in nature, but they'd laid just as much waste to the American landscape.

"Penelope?" Dillingham called.

"A minute, Paula," I snapped.

It was more like three. I didn't really need to wait that long; the worry I'd stoked had them reaching for their first glasses of wine before I closed the door of the head. They'd nearly emptied the bottle by the time I returned. I didn't take either player for lightweights. People like these two scumbags make a career out of drinking to excess and eating only the finest cuisine, some of it probably on the verge of extinction. They'd likely tried *Homo sapiens* during some of their less conventional buffets. I've heard that human flesh tastes like pork.

It was the first glass that concerned me.

"Penelope?" Cairo huffed, his words slurred at the edges.

Good. The Oxy was kicking in. Relief attempted to distract me.

"What the hell kind of game are you playing?"

"Oh, not so much a game as a bonanza," I said.

Dillingham narrowed her gaze. "You're not..."

"No," I said.

She rose up from one of those jizz-and-gore-soaked cushions, only to crash back down. Cairo took a little longer to succumb. I got into his face and was, surprisingly, shocked by the meanness in his eyes, the arrogance. The *evil*. What I do breaks one of the Commandments, but gets me out of jail free with the whole eye-for-an-eye rule. Him? I could tell he was comfortable with regularly breaking all ten.

"Who the fuck—?"

"I'm nobody," I said. "But I used to own a little house. Now, I'm just somebody who got put on the streets by you demons."

I swung the nearly empty bottle, and down Cairo went.

Over the intercom, I told the pilots there would be a slight delay and to hold tight. Then, with the help of my new friend the security guard, I dragged their unconscious bodies out and bound them to the landing gear. Not too tight. Not that, in a few hours when they woke, they wouldn't be able to loosen the knots, even unaware of exactly where they were in the deafening darkness.

I only cared that they got a clear look at the country they'd fucked over when the landing gear again lowered, thousands of feet above terra firma.

"You never saw me here," I said to my friend, the security guard.

"No," he said.

It was the truth. He didn't see me. He saw Pretty Penny, CEO and serial killer. Which was what I wanted.

I returned up the stairs, told the pilot to punch it and settled down for our expected five-hour flight. I didn't like the idea of being locked inside a tin can for that long, but amused myself by reliving the moment of impact between bottle and skull, which had left a nice bit of bloodied hair and scalp on the label, and helped myself to the snacks.

On approach to Boston, the landing gear lowered. I smiled, knowing we were still quite high up, high enough to give them a front row seat for what was to come. It truly was my crowning achievement. We landed. I left behind Penelope's ID and wallet—after emptying the latter of all cash, even the pennies and nickels. I hailed a taxi and headed north, toward the library, and none were ever the wiser.

* * *

How, you ask?

Gloves. Gloves are the key. That, and the almost stalwart belief that a woman isn't capable of committing that which I've turned into a profitable career. Hell, an art form! I don't know if that belief is misogynistic in nature, or a blessing. It helped me. I used it to my benefit. The world is a far better place without the murderous and psychotic lords and princesses I've liquidated; without so many cutthroat kings and queens that I've knocked from their thrones and who no longer cast shadows over the general populace. Some people should die. A lot of people. Most.

There's more I could tell you, but I think what you've read in my little manifesto speaks enough as to what was done to me and other innocents, and what I did in response to my oppressors, those former fucking ass-hats.

This manifesto...

I typed it up on the library computers. When I printed it up, side stapling it between card stock covers, I was careful to do so wearing gloves. Rule Number One, remember? It's not the best story ever told, but it sure is interesting, and one worth reading. I think the Wide Country part alone will become a blockbuster for Hollywood and a boon for one of those true crime writers. Any time two bodies plummet out of the sky and crash onto the streets of Greater Boston, the world is bound to take notice.

And so I wrote it all down.

Sure, they're looking for me. But the artist's rendering, well, they got it all wrong. I get a good laugh, though, and laughter's in too short supply in this ugly, new, post-Bush world.

From time to time, I leave a copy of this manifesto stuck between random books on various shelves. Oh, and so you know, I no longer live beneath the library stairs. I've got my own home again, a reasonable little place. I paid cash for it. I also run numerous charities, most benefiting the unemployed and homeless. I donate a lot of my profit to libraries too, because idiots and illiterates in power are always trying to slash their budgets and shut them down. Not as many anymore, mind you. You can probably guess why.

But I still love this library. Being here saved my life. I love to read. And the part of me that once wanted to be a writer loves to be read.

If you've read my manifesto this far, there's a good chance I'm somewhere close by, maybe sitting directly behind you. Go ahead and turn around. I dare you to.

Boo!

ABOUT THE AUTHOR
GREGORY L. NORRIS

Gregory L. Norris writes full-time from his home at the outer limits of New Hampshire.

He grew up on a healthy dose of creature double-features, and his work can be found in numerous national magazines and fiction anthologies. Norris has written for television, including *Star Trek: Voyager*. He is presently working with the Canadian production company, Space Opera Society, on various television and film projects.

AMPUTATIONS IN THE KEY OF D
JACK MADDOX

"Ah, Mr. Murder. Please, come in."

Daniel Murphy froze for a second before he stepped into the pristine, white office, struggling with an urge to chuckle. Under the stage name Danny Murder he'd sold sixteen million copies of his first album, *Fuck Struck Angels*, and his other four albums had each gone multiplatinum. He'd paraded on stage at Madison Square Garden in killer-mime makeup and sprayed a Super Soaker filled with goat's blood over a legion of Goth kids wailing his name.

And all it took to make him feel like a huge joke was someone addressing him in proper form: Mr. Murder. Husband of Mrs. Murder. Father of sweet little Baby Murder.

Sweet Little Baby Murder? There's a world tour in that, he thought.

There were two doctors, both seated at either end of something more like a dining room table than a desk. The table was piled high with anatomy books, scribbled papers, manila folders bulging with patient records, paper plates covered in chocolate crumbs, and a human heart floating in a jar of formaldehyde. Daniel didn't find the organ's presence strange at all. He had a collection of his own at home, mostly kidneys and brains picked up cheap on the Internet.

The doctors, on the other hand...*quite* strange. You could tell they were doctors because they were wearing white coats. Beyond that, there was nothing very medical about them. It would have been a hard fight just to make it to hygienic.

The doctor who'd greeted him was, not to put too fine a point on it, very fat. Rolls of fat in his neck quivered like a Jell-O mold. Whenever he shifted his enormous ass, the chair beneath him squeaked in agony. His gray slacks were stretched out like sausage casings. The nametag pinned to the lapel of his white coat read "DR. AURICLE" in tiny, black letters. His eyes peered out from the mounds of flesh hanging from his face, two greedy little blue marbles.

The other doctor...he was certainly there, but Daniel couldn't quite focus on him; his eyes kept reflexively bouncing away to the floor, or to one of the many framed certificates lining the walls. All he came away with memory-wise was a set of eyes that were green as river ice and a name tag that read "DR. ROSTRUM." Maybe he was a ghost, something Daniel had no problem with; he'd bought his extravagant Beverly Hills mansion because it was the site of a famous axe murder back in the Roaring Twenties.

With a sausage finger, Dr. Auricle gestured at an empty chair. "Please have a seat, sir, and may I say you have a very interesting idea of what music is."

Daniel sat with his eyes narrowed, caught off guard by the doctor's comment. "What?"

Dr. Auricle's pudgy hand dove into the clutter on the desk and came up with a CD case, the cover art depicting a smiling suburban mother serving diced-up rats to her family for breakfast. It was *All-American Tragedies*, another multiplatinum album that had been universally slammed by the critics, mostly because he'd chosen to play lead guitar himself and ended up producing the musical equivalent of a drunken orgy—messy, complicated and emotionally unsatisfying.

Daniel just shrugged, a slender young man in faded jeans and a white button-down shirt. His skin was quite tanned, the result of spending up to forty hours a week lying on one beach or another. Mime-faced Danny Murder was just a character on a stage, someone who couldn't be hurt by newspaper clippings that said he had no talent.

The problem was Danny was just that. A character. And it was getting easier to back away from him these days.

"So, you guys listen to a lot of death metal around here?" Daniel asked.

Dr. Auricle gave a hearty laugh while Dr. Rostrum sat and stared with those icy eyes. "We usually stick with Bach and Mozart," the fat man said, "but we didn't want to be *completely* unfamiliar with your work. It's been a long time since Dr. Rostrum and I met a famous musician, hasn't it, Doctor?"

"Gentleman from Black Sabbath," Dr. Rostrum said. "Last I remember." His voice was so quiet that Daniel almost believed he'd just heard it in his head.

"Still," said Dr. Auricle with a broad grin that revealed a set of white, and perfectly even, false teeth, "the medical field has given us a wide variety of talented people to work on. Painters, actors, gymnasts, poets, inventors. No one is safe from their own body, are they, Mr. Murder?"

"Please don't call me that," Daniel said, pushing a lock of long, black hair behind his ear. "It makes me sound like a Stephen King novel or something."

Dr. Auricle laughed again. He rolled his chair away from the desk and leaned far enough into Daniel's personal space to show the tracks of pink skin beneath his thinning hair. "I believe that a former patient of ours recommended us. Exactly what did she tell you, Mr. Murder?"

Her name was Samantha, one of his groupies. Her left arm was missing at the shoulder, but that didn't stop her from being one of his favorite playmates. She'd lost the arm in a car accident, she claimed, and these two had patched her up.

"*You'll get along with them,*" Samantha said somewhere in the back of his memory. "*They're artists.*"

He shrugged. "Nah, found you guys in the phone book."

Dr. Auricle nodded. "Well then, pleasantries aside, I suppose we should have a look at the problem."

Daniel hesitated, looked down at the black leather gloves on his hands.

"Come, come," said Dr. Auricle. He leaned back and folded his arms over his massive chest. "We can't help you until you believe we can, Mr. Murder."

Daniel sighed and tugged the glove off his right hand, pointed his index finger at them like it was a gun. "There. You can see it. Satisfied?"

Dr. Auricle cocked his head to the side, eyes narrowing, making an interested *hmmm* sound. From the pocket of his white coat, he took a pair of the most elaborate eyeglasses Daniel had ever seen then slipped them on, black frames armed with several sets of magnifying lenses that enlarged his eyes to the size of oranges. "A healthy specimen of *Verruca vulgaris*, otherwise known as the common wart."

The w-word sliced through Daniel's heart like a spear. He waited patiently while the doctor took his hand, turning it this way and that. The wart was on the middle joint of his index finger, big, dark brown and misshapen. Three hairs grew out of it like spider legs.

It was the one dark spot of Daniel Murphy's life.

"So tell me, Mr. Murder," Dr. Auricle said, "why do you want this *blemish*, for lack of a more delicate term, removed?"

Daniel shrugged. "I'm not a big fan of being a circus freak, that's all."

"My boy, this is hardly the biggest disfigurement my associate and I have ever seen. Take one Mr. Joseph Merrick, for example."

"Lovely conversationalist," Dr. Rostrum said, "and a wonderful cricketer."

"A gentleman who suffered from perhaps history's worst case of neurofibromatosis, causing extreme skeletal disfiguration, as well as huge growths that caused him to resemble an elephant with one tusk. Also one of the most gifted and intelligent minds we've had cause to encounter."

"Yeah, and he died back in eighteen-ninety," Daniel said. He knew his David Lynch movies. "You trying to tell me that you two met him over a hundred years ago?"

Dr. Auricle laughed and slapped his meaty side. "No, no, my

boy! I mean we actually encountered his brain, on auction in Europe. Would've made a wonderful addition to my collection, but for the Colombian drug lord who ended up swiping it. But I digress. No, I was simply musing on the nature of what modern society perceives as imperfections. How people who are afflicted by disfigurement are often seen as helpless, even inferior, when in fact, it often seems that the lesser the person, the greater potential for talent."

Daniel wasn't impressed. He'd been in Hollywood for five years now. Philosophy didn't go over well in a twenty-minute town. "Listen, I really need to get going. Can we hurry up and just cut the son of a bitch off, or freeze it off, or whatever it is you do? I promise you can keep the damn thing afterwards, stare at it all you want, but I have places to go and people to do."

"Well, we've come a long way from just 'cutting the son of a bitch off,' Mr. Murder," Dr. Auricle said, unfazed. "We can't rush an operation that could potentially damage your hand's fine motor skills. After all, you couldn't play your guitar shy of a digit, could you?"

Daniel snorted. "I've played it with my dick. Sounds the same either way."

Dr. Auricle looked at him over the tops of his glasses. No, he *examined* him, as he would examine a slide crawling with interesting bacteria under a microscope. "Sir, music is, after all, your business. Your bread and butter, one might say. Do you really not care about your own talent that much?"

Daniel pursed his lips into a small smile. It would have been more at home on the face of some long-haired juvenile delinquent seated at the back of a remedial math class, a kid who thought skateboards and fart jokes were the best things in life, who could look forward to a long life of pumping gas and chasing stray dogs before shuffling off from cigarette-assisted suicide at age fifty.

No matter which face it was on, that smile said the same thing: *I don't care, and there's nothing you can say to make me.*

Dr. Auricle nodded curtly and said, "We'll schedule the operation for tomorrow. Soon enough, Mr. Murder, all of your troubles will be at an end."

* * *

The operating room was a blinding white. Nurses scuttled to and fro in their whites. Too many nurses for something as small as a wart removal, Daniel thought.

He sat on the operating table feeling foolish. They'd put one of the puffy plastic bags over his head, and he was wearing a white hospital gown that revealed the tattoo of a cherub brandishing a machine gun on his left ass cheek, done way back in the early days, touring with Twincest. He could still remember Lucky and Max in the background, laughing as a great big, sweating biker stamped ink into his ass forever. After that he'd sworn off tequila for a whole week.

Dr. Auricle appeared with his face covered by a surgeon's mask so only his greedy little eyes showed. Daniel flipped onto his back, wincing as the cold metal touched skin. "Listen, Doc, I was wondering why there were so many—"

"So many nurses?" Dr. Auricle gave a fatherly chuckle. "Insurance companies, my boy. Your insurer seems to feel that my associate and I may make off with a piece of the famous Danny Murder.

Ridiculous of course, but in our profession we've discovered one cannot have too many witnesses. Ah, here comes the notary."

A tubby little man in a black suit slapped a pile of papers onto Daniel's chest and stuck a pen in his hand. He riffled through the pages until he found a dotted line and said, "Sign here."

Daniel did.

More riffling. "And here."

Daniel did.

"And initial here."

He did.

The little man in black vanished.

Daniel shook his head. Nothing pissed him off more than when people waved papers in his face to sign, another hazard of being rich and famous. He had an appearance down at the Viper Room scheduled for that evening, a recording session the next day and a whole life to look forward to after that. Hanging around this nuthouse wasn't on the agenda.

He was quite surprised when Dr. Rostrum appeared and lowered an anesthetic mask over his face. He opened his mouth to protest, inhaled a lungful of sodium pentothal, and suddenly the operating room seemed to be receding into the distance.

Somewhere off in that dark haze he heard Dr. Auricle saying, "Normally, Mr. Murder, we would use a local anesthetic for something like a wart removal. The whole procedure would be done in a little over fifteen minutes. Then again, where's the fun in that?"

* * *

When he came to and found himself in the recovery room, arms and legs heavy as lead, right hand swathed in bandages, he'd learn that his latest single, "Hometown Hatred," written for his father, a Pentecostal minister who'd organized protest rallies and CD burnings for his only son's work, had risen to the number one spot on the charts, for both radio play and downloads.

Within five minutes, none of that was going to matter.

Dr. Auricle sat on the bed beside him, making the mattress bow under his weight. He was smiling like a cat with a big, fat mouse trapped under its paw. Someone that might have been Dr. Rostrum and might have been an empty white coat lurked behind him

"How are we feeling, Mr. Murder?" Dr. Auricle inquired.

Daniel's mouth felt stuffed with cotton. "Hnnnnng."

"Glad to hear it. Unfortunately, not all of the news is of the, as you say, *'good'* variety."

"HNNNNG!"

"As you say. Well, Mr. Murder, the normal process for wart removal is a fairly simple one. It would have involved me, as attending surgeon, first administering a local anesthetic that would have numbed the index finger, followed by a small incision to remove the specimen. A stitch or two later, and you would have been fit as a fiddle. Or, in your case, a Warlock electric guitar." He chuckled at his own joke. "Then there are other methods, such as freezing or burning that could result in considerably more pain, but would still not be too difficult for specialists such as ourselves."

"Hnnnng?"

"Perhaps. Well, sometimes, in the medical profession, mistakes are made. Clerical errors happen. Slippery notaries provide misleading paperwork. And sometimes the mistakes are only discovered long after anything can be done to fix them."

"HNNNNG?!"

"Which is a long way of saying that things haven't gone quite as planned. But hey, this *is* what God gave us health insurance for."

He produced a small pair of scissors and cut the bandages away from Daniel's hand. Daniel somehow found the strength to turn his head.

When he saw his index finger was missing, the stump stitched closed with black surgical thread, he found it much easier to scream.

* * *

In the week that followed, Daniel Murphy was rarely seen leaving his mansion in west Beverly Hills, and the few times he did he always wore a black glove on his right hand, the empty finger drooping miserably.

Daniel's lawyer, Kyle Roth, hit the roof when he heard. He spent five days screaming at hospital administrators over the phone, and had informed Daniel, lying in his king-sized bed looking malnourished and pale, of four things:

First, the hospital that employed Drs. Auricle and Rostrum claimed that the paperwork Daniel had signed clearly outlined the procedure of removing an index finger and would have been noted by the patient had he read the papers carefully. Daniel himself stayed silent for this part.

Second, there was no small, overweight notary in a black suit employed by that hospital.

Third, nobody employed by said hospital knew what had become of Daniel's finger.

And lastly, no administrator employed by said hospital was going to have a clean pair of underwear left after Kyle Roth finished suing them into oblivion.

"I mean, can you believe this shit?" Roth said in Daniel's general direction as he leafed through some papers. Daniel didn't respond, had already learned that when Kyle spoke he might as well have been talking to himself in a mirror. "First they slip the wrong paperwork into their files, and now they refuse to give any information on the doctors. They won't show employment records, tax information, testimonies from prior patients. This is going to be one thorough stomping, I can tell you that. Am I right? You get some rest, big guy. We're all counting on you."

Throughout all of his meetings with Roth, with the mansion's staff, with his agent, and with the New Age guru Roth had insisted on calling in for "spiritual healing"—as if a gently smiling Japanese gentleman burning incense and talking about the healing power of herbal tea was going to magically re-grow his fucking finger—Daniel did none of the talking. He stayed in his room, every so often lurching to the mini-bar to medicate himself with Southern Comfort.

He wasn't manically depressed, like the tabloids claimed, and he wasn't considering legal strategies, like Roth and his agent claimed.

He wasn't even angry with the doctors.

He stayed up late writing lyrics. No music, not yet—and he figured it would be a lot of fun composing with a missing digit when he got that far, har-de-har—but the words came pouring out of him, filling up entire notebooks with his messy handwriting. He wrote about highways at sunset, about the secret names of cats, about the stars just being dancers on the dark floor of the night.

He only now realized how much he'd been thinking about a wart.

Ever since his agents had hired a lyricist to do the songs—Daniel losing time to partying and groupies and special appearances—he had forgotten how it felt to stroll through a garden made of words. It was so easy, even with the missing stump of your finger bleeding through the bandages.

Maybe he'd forgotten that blood went into music more often than anybody thought.

* * *

On the morning of the seventh day, a phone call.

"Danny, my boy, some great news from the front lines."

"What's up, Kyle?"

"We finally cut through the red tape at the hospital. They found the finger in cold storage, and they're pretty sure they can reattach it. So first we get your finger back, and then we cheerfully stomp their asses in court. Am I right?"

Long silence.

"Danny? You still there?"

"Yeah, I'm here. I was just wondering...did they find out what happened to those doctors?"

Roth chuckled. "They must've run for the border after you checked out of the hospital. Doesn't matter. We've got the administrators by the balls. I mean, I know what they did to you, but did you really want to see *them* again?"

Another pause. "Well, maybe I wanted to, you know, thank them."

Roth burst out laughing. "God, you crazy fuck. I thought you being nuts was just an act."

* * *

That night, Daniel awoke from a dream. He'd been rolling through brightly lit hallways in a wheelchair, one of the big, old-fashioned ones made of wood, and the wheels had squeaked with every turn. He passed by rooms with horrible things happening inside. Body parts all over the place. Hands. Feet. Organs. Bones still stained with blood. And music had been playing somewhere.

He rubbed his eyes and the dream melted away. Everything except that music. He sat up in bed and looked around at the prison he'd built for himself.

There were posters on the walls from all of his concerts and world tours. Danny Murder, clad in black leather, his face contorted and screaming. Danny Murder throwing fake severed heads into the crowd. Danny Murder cutting himself onstage with razor blades. And now, thinking back, he supposed it was his own father who'd shown him the correct methods of terrorizing an audience into paying attention.

Dear old Terrence Scarborough Murphy, lifelong servant of the Pentecostal Church, snake handler and strychnine drinker. His father had told him that he was going to Hell because of his music. Daniel wondered if his father knew that you could go to Hell without even knowing.

He wondered if he was now figuring that out for himself.

A long, black guitar case waited in the corner of his closet, lightly coated with dust. Inside was a classic 1965 Gibson Les Paul, cream-and-red, scrolled with mahogany. It had never been played.

Daniel spent a while trying to remember how to tune it. It was like being back at the beginning, back when he'd formed a band with his friends from high school, a couple of crazy guys named Mad Max and Lucky.

They'd called themselves Twincest, Max on drums, Lucky on lead vocals, and Daniel on guitar, playing taverns and nightclubs for fifty bucks a night. Even when they got chased out of town by potbellied rednecks wearing John Deere caps and denim jackets, even when their old VW bus had broken down in the middle of the Nevada desert and Lucky had to walk ten miles to get to a phone, there was the sweet tang of steel strings.

That was before he had learned he was the best-looking of the group, before he forgot the music, choosing instead to concentrate on the girls, the reputation, and before he started looking for an agent and a label.

The last time he'd spoken to Lucky was just before his first show at Madison Square Garden. The connection crackled with static and Lucky's voice, rolling and sonorous, always the real singer of the two of them, sounded like it was coming from the dark side of the moon: *"Dude, it doesn't matter you filled the Garden. You're playing to an empty room. And you always will."*

He'd heard that Twincest was still together, rounded out by a few chicks who played piano and tambourine or some shit like that, still working small venues in the middle of nowhere. They had the music. He had the millions of adoring fans, the money, and the rock-star cliché of sex, drugs and rock 'n' roll. And he was still playing to an empty room.

By the time he finished tuning the Les Paul it felt like a shard of hot glass was being slowly driven into his bandaged hand.

He began playing the tune from his dream. It started slow, his numb fingers finding their own way. He hammered the strings, the notes swelling and receding, not at all affected by the mute sound of an unplugged guitar.

He finished fifteen minutes later. His stump had bled through the bandages, and droplets of blood had spattered the front of the guitar in a spray. He felt just fine.

* * *

He was wheeled into the same room where they'd removed the finger in the first place. Some of the same nurses were there. At some point the doctors had shown Daniel his finger, lying at the bottom of a little silver tray like a sausage.

He just nodded silently when he saw it. It was just a finger, looked like it could belong on anybody's hand.

He lay on the operating table, looking up at the bright lights, letting the noises of the room fade to a comfortable buzz in the background. It felt like waiting for a performance to start, the distant rumbling of the crowd...

"So glad to see you again, Mr. Murder."

Daniel craned his head to the left. Dr. Auricle peered down at him.

"Am I dreaming?" Daniel asked. He felt quite calm.

The doctor shrugged. "Your guess is as good as mine. Dr. Rostrum and myself have been here quite some time, on the edges of things. Sometimes folks like yourself slip in with us. No rhyme or reason to the whole process." His familiar rumbling laugh. "On the whole, I think I prefer medicine over metaphysics. Everything neatly labeled and categorized."

He walked over to a dusty, cobwebbed relay with a switch the length of a man's forearm. Dr. Auricle threw the relay. The sound of monstrous gears grinding together roared under the floor, and the operating room began to turn a slow axis.

Daniel moved his head, looked around the room. Dr. Rostrum was there, pulling medical tools from a big, black doctor's bag with brass clasps. The tools were old, rusty, unlike anything Daniel had ever seen. They were made to extract, cut or separate while inflicting enough pain to drive someone mad.

The fat doctor stood beside Daniel, the white light bathing him, making him an obscene parody of an angel. Daniel was too awed to move. He licked his lips and said, "Are you...what are you?"

Dr. Auricle snapped on a pair of white latex gloves. "Once upon a time, we were ordinary surgeons. Back when the plague-carts carried heaps of bodies to the lime pits, we were there studying the limits of flesh, amounts of pain that could be endured, cures that killed more often than not. A horrid time, the plague, another end of the world for our patients to suffer through, and we were there to mend their bodies when they reached the breaking point. But we grew disillusioned with the body, which is nothing more than a brilliant machine destined to rot away into dust, and instead began to focus on the spirit, and along the way we performed some...unwise experiments on our own spiritual states. But through all we've experienced, a single question has driven us. The question that Dr. Rostrum and I are attempting to answer is simple: If a talented mind has no connection to the body, will the talent sustain itself?"

He no longer seemed to be speaking to Daniel, who finally realized the room had stopped turning.

Somewhere past the lights, Daniel could see he was no longer in an operating room, but an operating *theater*. Balconies were arranged all around the chamber, filled with men in black suits. Some of them peered through opera glasses. There were hundreds of them, and to each and every one he was not a human with dreams and feelings.

He was a test subject. A number on a form. A cadaver-to-be.

He heard the scritch-scratch of pens on expensive vellum paper.

What do all those nurses and the "real" doctors see back in the "real" world? he thought in the depth of his panic. *They see a talentless man lying unconscious on an operating table. And when I wake up, who will have performed the operation?*

He knew. The real doctors had already taken his finger. Now they were getting ready to take something else.

Dr. Auricle laid a cool hand on Daniel's forehead. "Yes, you could see it as us taking something from you. Did you see it that way when you played the song from your dream last night?"

Daniel was silent. The eyeless nurses belted his arms and legs down with heavy, leather straps. He stayed silent as the table flipped and rotated, came to rest with him facing Dr. Auricle, limbs spread in the position of Da Vinci's Vitruvian Man.

Dr. Auricle snapped his fingers and the little, grinning notary appeared, his black suit pressed, polished grin shining in the white lights. He began scribbling on a clipboard while Dr. Auricle spoke.

"Subject is a Caucasian male, approximately twenty-three years of age, no identifying marks or scars, except for a rather unseemly tattoo on his left buttock. Despite his claims of being a musician, his right hand shows no calluses of the skin, nor any of the muscle build formed by use of stringed musical instruments. The subject is delusional to the point that he believed that a wart was the worst thing that could ever happen to him. However, quiet surveillance has shown the subject to have had a positive response to the first step of the treatment. Therefore, we begin step two."

He dropped the formal speak, and while Dr. Rostrum wheeled the cart bearing its ugly surgical tools towards them, he whispered into Daniel's ear:

"I believe that Samantha was the patient who brought you to us, Mr. Murder. Funny, she always dreamed of being a ballerina. At the time she was a heroin addict who needed a tattoo removed, the name of an old lover as I recall. Then we treated her. She was upset at first...until she realized that the loss of her arm gave her perfect poise and balance. That is what we do, Mr. Murder. We perfected her. She is now one of the finest dancers the world will ever know. But *you*, my boy...much work is needed. We plan to reawaken your mind's desire for music, by making your body less of a distraction. The greater the work, the greater the reward. You will be our masterpiece."

He bent down to the cart and came up with a rusty scalpel in one hand and a bone saw in the other.

Daniel was almost grateful when the anesthetic mask was pressed over his mouth.

* * *

He woke expecting to see Dr. Auricle again but it was just Roth, looking down at him with an expression that was both concerned and anxious. His fingers were twiddling with the gold chain that never seemed to leave his neck. "Heya, boss," he said. "I told the staff to leave us alone for this. Figured you wouldn't like anybody around."

"Around for what?" Daniel mumbled. "I'm not really in shape for a concert."

Roth gave a tittering laugh. It was the laugh of a man who knows that if he doesn't laugh he might start crying, and if he starts crying he might never stop. "No, it's just that...." He trailed off and tried again. "They claim they made another clerical error, and...." He trailed off again, groping blindly for inspiration. "Listen, I'm gonna nail these fuckers to the fucking wall. Nobody can do this shit to the same person twice."

He finished by bursting into tears and sinking down to the floor on his ass. It took a lot for a lawyer like Kyle Roth to cry like a little girl in front of his biggest client.

Like maybe if his client's entire right hand had been surgically removed, the stump stitched closed with black thread. That would do it.

Daniel looked at the stump, then looked at Roth. His eyes were bright.

"Get me to the studio," he said.

* * *

Snapshots of Daniel Murphy in the months that followed:

- 1 -

Daniel sits in the recording studio, putting the finishing touches on a new single, "Falling to Pieces." The producers shake their heads in amazement, and the backup band can hardly stay focused.

Danny Murder is no longer screaming into the microphone like an animal, like Jim Morrison did before he was found in that apartment in Paris, cold and alone. He has the voice of an angel. He sings about a heart breaking to pieces, of a girl with one arm who put the pieces back together and sealed them with a kiss.

He can no longer play guitar himself, not with the missing right hand, along with the thumb that's been amputated from the left.

- 2 -

A concert in Las Vegas, Nevada, four weeks later.

The fans aren't chanting "DAAANNY! DAAANNY!" as they always did before. No, the wannabe children of the night, the little kids playing dress-up in their black lipstick and Mommy's eye shadow, they might as well have been hypnotized.

Danny Murder is wearing no face paint, no flames spurting from the stage around him. He's accompanied by the lonely sound of a single piano, and he sings about loss. He sings about losing yourself, and finding yourself. The fans are almost as touched by this as they are horrified by how he's vanishing a little bit at a time.

Daniel Murphy is in a wheelchair, both feet removed at the ankle, and a black patch covers his empty right eye socket.

- 3 -

One morning he wheels himself out of his bedroom—it cost quite a lot to renovate, but the whole house is now wheelchair-accessible—and sees something on the floor. It's a red rose, fully bloomed, the thorns clipped from the long, green stem.

He picks it up with his withered left hand and reads the small paper wound around the stem. It's written in fluid calligraphy, and all it says is: *I'm sorry. Samantha.*

He'd had Roth check in on her now and then. A week earlier he had learned she was going to New York. A place for lovely ballet dancers, even the ones missing arms. He refolds the paper, kisses it and says, "You don't have to be," to no one in particular.

- 4 -

At some point he wakes up in the hospital and realizes everything they've done, everything he *agreed to let them do*, and he screams at Dr. Auricle. "WHY? FOR GOD'S SAKE WHY ARE YOU DOING THIS?!!!"

Dr. Auricle peels off his bloody gloves. He's not surprised by this reaction; he's seen everything from complete psychotic breakdowns to divine visions—which sometimes turned out to be pretty much the same thing. He is serene as ever when he replies, "Because one day you'll thank us for this."

- 5 -

The operations become more frequent. In between his Hall of Fame induction and winning a Grammy for Best Rock Album—neither of which he is present for—Daniel learns what it's like to have your circulatory system removed. He gets the privilege of seeing his own heart beating inside a jar. He also learns that one can only see Dr. Rostrum when one's eyes have been scooped out. He finally sees the green-eyed doctor, and what he sees tips him into an almost perfect madness. He composes a sixteen-minute concerto about the experience and calls it "Black Hole Sonata."

- 6 -

Danny Murder's slow disappearance is not noted by the media, and despite the universal critical praise for his last album, *Dirge*, he has almost completely vanished from the charts. His mansion goes up for sale three years later.

An unusual find is made when a small safe is opened in the wall of the master bedroom: notebooks full of unpublished songs and poems, most of them concerning a ballet dancer from the East Coast named Samantha Graynor, who declines to comment when the songs are leaked online. Others are written in a different hand from Daniel Murphy's, the lyrics requiring almost as much translation as Egyptian hieroglyphs.

One musical historian working on the notebooks makes a small joke. "Musicians and doctors are the only people with such shitty handwriting."

The songs themselves are dark, much darker than Daniel's previous work. The historian who made the handwriting joke reads them for several weeks, and then is committed to a sanitarium "for his own safety."

* * *

On the other side:
From deep within the hospital's basement, a young man sang.

A little maiden climbed an old man's knees—
Begged for a story: "Do uncle, please!
Why are you single, why live alone?
Have you no babies, have you no home?"
"I had a sweetheart, years, years ago,
Where she is now, pet, you will soon know;
List to the story, I'll tell it all:
I believed her faithless after the ball."

The operating theater was being scrubbed down in preparation for new patients. A janitor's mop slapped the floor, smearing blood and shit on the white tiles. He hummed along with the tune. Soon, his fellow grey, stony, lifeless workers picked it up, and the great theater shook with the sound.

"Bright lights were flashing in the grand ballroom,
Softly the music playing sweet tunes.
There came my sweetheart, my love, my own,
'I wish some water; leave me alone.'
When I returned, dear, there stood a man
Kissing my sweetheart as lovers can.
Down fell the glass, pet, broken, that's all—
Just as my heart was after the ball."

The corridors twisted and turned, passing by cells that contained other geniuses waiting for their talents to be released, men and women crying and muttering to themselves, sometimes drawing idyllic landscapes or writing epic poems on the walls, using their own blood for ink.

Finally, the long, twisting journey ended at the laboratory. Dr. Rostrum's particular passion, where he hoped to someday reverse the curious experiment he once performed on himself, the one that had left him more shade than flesh. Now, the room with its bubbling jars full of eyeballs and steaming beakers and things tap-tap-tapping on the walls of their glass cages, now it had become a studio.

> "Long years have passed, child, I've never wed,
> True to my lost love though she is dead.
> She tried to tell me, tried to explain—
> I would not listen, pleadings were vain.
> One day a letter came from that man;
> He was her brother, the letter ran.
> That's why I'm lonely, no home at all—
> I broke her heart, pet, after the ball."

Daniel Murphy's head rested in a jar of Dr. Rostrum's special electrified saline solution. A metal collar bound around his neck fed electricity from two copper wires inserted into the top of his spinal column. His head was shaved, his eyes removed, but his tongue and vocal cords had been enhanced by all of Auricle and Rostrum's considerable surgical skill.

Electrodes were attached to his scalp, and the printer they were connected to showed something remarkable. The subject, no longer distracted by petty flesh, was now able to compose up to twelve incredibly complex songs *simultaneously*. The musical notes came scritch-scratching out of the printer at an almost frightening pace. Daniel's new voice came spilling from a brass horn on the side of the jar, something you'd see on an old wind-up phonograph.

Sometimes it devolved into senseless screaming, but the artificial lungs across the room were designed to suppress a certain amount of sound, so that the doctors' workplace would never be disturbed.

The only sounds besides his singing were the steady *beep-beep-beep* of a heart monitor, the bubbling of the saline jar.

"After the ball is over, after the break of morn,
After the dancers' leaving, after the stars are gone,
Many a heart is aching, if you could read them all,
Many the hopes that have vanished after the ball.
Many the hopes that have vanished after the ball."

Dr. Auricle and Dr. Rostrum observed the head through the glass of its little prison. When it finally fell silent, they both gave a polite smattering of applause.

"I do wish he'd stop singing that over and over," said Dr. Auricle. "Gives me the creeping willies. But if all else fails, at least the young fellow has come to appreciate the classics." He turned to his partner. "Well, I suppose the time has come to move Mr. Murder into the final phase."

Dr. Rostrum consulted a clipboard and grunted. "Complete separation of brain from remaining cranium. Subject will continue to operate on neural stimuli alone. Remaining cranium will be kept in cold storage for possible recycling."

Dr. Auricle nodded gravely, and his fat hand caressed the side of the jar, admired the innocent smile on what was left of Daniel Murphy's face.

"Better get to it then. We have things to do. Artists to free."

They set off to prepare the operating theater, leaving behind the fading echoes of a lonely song.

ABOUT THE AUTHOR
JACK MADDOX

Jack Maddox learned how to write by watching old *Tales From the Crypt* episodes. His work has been featured in *Dark Moon Digest 10* and the upcoming anthology *The Last Diner*. His first novel, *The Dog: Necrophagus*, is forthcoming from Necro Publications/Bedlam Press.

There are many terrible things in his head.

HOUSESITTING
RAY GARTON

Darlene left her house at a few minutes after nine in the morning, went across the street to the Cullpeppers' and let herself in with the key they had given her. It was a crisp, fall morning and she wore a heavy wool sweater of forest green, a pair of jeans and tennis shoes.

Nancy Cullpepper's aunt Eva had died and she and her husband Harold had gone north to Medford, Oregon to bury her. They had left two days ago and would be back tomorrow. Darlene and her husband, Ralph, had agreed to housesit, although it was Darlene, of course, who did the work. Nancy had insisted on paying the going housesitting rate, whatever that might be.

"It's a chore," Nancy had said, "so I insist on paying you. I mean, even though it's only three days, it's still a terrible inconvenience for you. You have to come over twice a day to feed and water the cats and the iguana. You have to clean out the litter boxes. I *insist* on paying you."

Darlene felt strange taking money for it because they had known the Cullpeppers for so long and were such good friends. Nancy was her best friend in the world. Housesitting for them just seemed like something they should do, something the Cullpeppers would certainly do for them if the situation were reversed. Of course, Darlene and Ralph didn't have four cats and an iguana.

It was strange being in their house alone. Somehow, the empty silence was not welcoming. Two of the cats—Rosie, a sleek Abyssinian, and Buster, a gray tabby with white socks—met her at the door when she came in. The other two—Maxie, a moody Siamese, and Carmen, a Persian—were more skittish and tended to keep to themselves. She bent down and petted them, talked to them a little.

Darlene went to the kitchen, to the door that led out to the garage. It had a kitty-door built into the bottom of it so the cats could go through. Their food and litter boxes were kept out there. In the garage, she opened a couple of cans of Friskies and spooned the food onto their plates, poured some dry food into the bowl. She took their water bowl into the kitchen and freshened it, scooped out the two litter boxes and put in some fresh sand.

Back in the kitchen, she went to the refrigerator, reached into the resealable bag in the crisper and got a handful of greens for Wallet, Harold's iguana. She took the greens down the hall to Harold's office, where they kept the lizard's large terrarium. The green lizard gave Darlene the creeps, so she did not enjoy reaching into the terrarium to put food in its bowl. But Wallet seemed to feel the same way about her and backed away from her hand each time she reached in. She took the water bowl out and across the hall to the bathroom to refill it, then put it back.

She had a headache that throbbed at her temples. She'd had a fight with Ralph that morning. She couldn't even remember what it was about. Something stupid. She left Harold's office, closed the door, and stood there in the hall, thinking, trying to remember what the fight had been about. She had neglected to wash the shirt Ralph had wanted to wear to work that day, that was it. Such a stupid thing. But it seemed they fought over stupid things quite a lot lately.

Part of it was that Ralph was unhappy at his job. He was general manager at Circuit Breakers, an electronics store. The chain was cutting back and there was a lot of tension because no one knew if the store would be closed. Everyone was afraid, polishing their resumes just in case.

Ralph had been against the idea of housesitting for the Cullpeppers at first. "What if something goes wrong?" he'd said. "What if one of the cats gets sick and dies? Even if it's not your fault, if it happens while you're taking care of them, it's your responsibility. Or what if that damned lizard of Harold's dies? Anything could happen, you never know. It's like loaning money between friends, it's the kind of thing that could damage the friendship." She had assured him nothing like that would happen. It was only three days, after all. He'd gone along with it in the end.

Darlene went across the hall to the bathroom and looked in the medicine cabinet to see if there was something she could take for her headache. All she had at home was Tylenol, and that never worked for her. Some *real* aspirin would do the trick. But the cabinet contained no medicine.

She went down the hall to the master bedroom and into the bathroom there. It was much larger than the one in the hall, with two sinks, a medicine cabinet over each. She checked the first cabinet and found a bottle of Vicodin. She shook two into her palm and replaced the bottle. She removed a Dixie Cup from the dispenser on the wall and drank the pills down with cold tap water, then crushed the cup and tossed it into the small garbage can under the sink.

Darlene left the bathroom and sat on the edge of the king-size bed. Curled up at the foot of the bed, Carmen looked up for a moment with sleepy eyes. She reached over and gently stroked the Persian. Carmen purred. Darlene looked at the pictures of the Cullpepper children on the wall. In one framed photograph, Kristine wore her cap and gown and held her high-school diploma. She was attending Stanford now, studying speech pathology. Beside it was a photograph of their son, Lewis, at his college graduation. He was married, living down in the Bay Area, serving his internship at a small law firm in San Raphael.

Ralph was sterile from a childhood case of the mumps. They had looked into adoption, but had never followed through with it. Darlene had never felt any great yearning for children, but she often wondered what their life would have been like with them. They would be grown now, like the Cullpeppers' children, and she and Ralph would be alone anyway.

She stood and went over to Nancy's closet and browsed through her clothes. Nancy was a paralegal and a snappy dresser. She was svelte, with a figure Darlene envied. Darlene was not overweight, but clothes never looked as good on her as they did on Nancy.

She went from the closet to Nancy's dresser and opened a bottle of perfume. She sniffed it, rubbed a little on her wrist. She opened the top drawer. Underwear. She opened the next drawer. Sweaters folded and stacked neatly. Cashmere. She took one out and rubbed it against her cheek a few times, then put it back. She closed the drawer, bent down, and opened the next one.

A quick chill passed over her. *What am I doing?* she thought. She suddenly felt like a child doing something naughty. It was not exactly a bad feeling. It had a certain thrill to it.

There were some small cardboard boxes in the drawer. She took one out and opened it. It contained a collection of lapel buttons that bore slogans. One read: "SO, WHEN IS THE WIZARD GOING TO GET BACK TO YOU ABOUT THAT BRAIN?" Darlene chuckled and looked at another. In dripping red letters: "WANNA COME UP AND SEE MY CHAINSAW?" There were dozens more in the box. She didn't know Nancy collected buttons. She wondered how old the collection was, when she'd started.

She put the box back and opened another. She gasped. It contained Polaroid snapshots of Nancy in lingerie, some of her naked.

"Oh, my," Darlene said with a smirk.

She felt a pang of guilt mingled with a frisson of excitement.

"You're a bad girl, Nancy," she whispered as she browsed through the photos.

There were some pictures of Harold, too. He was a large man, six-four, broad-shouldered with a deep chest. But he was less than well-endowed. Harold was an insurance salesman, white and doughy from too much time spent indoors at a desk.

She came to a few pictures of them together: holding each other, fondling, playing, all smiles. Darlene wondered if someone else had been there to take them, or if they'd managed to take the pictures themselves.

A thump in the living room startled her so badly she dropped the pictures and they scattered over the floor. She quickly gathered them up and put them back in the box, put the box back in the drawer, and closed it. She left the bedroom and hurried down the hall.

Rosie and Buster were rolling around on the living room floor, rough-housing. Darlene sighed with relief.

She'd had only a banana for breakfast and was hungry, so she went to the kitchen to find something to eat. On the counter by the toaster she found a box of Little Debbie donuts and took one, bit into it. She knew she should leave, but there was no compelling reason for her to go back home. She worked at an answering service, but it was her day off. She had laundry to do, but nothing else. She wanted to make sure she had Ralph's shirt washed and ready for tomorrow by the time he got home so he would have nothing to complain about. She hoped his mood was better when he returned from work.

She finished the donut and got another from the box, took it with her back down the hall to the bedroom. She was reminded of the time as a girl when she had sneaked into her older sister's bedroom and read her diary. There was something exciting about snooping through someone else's things, something almost erotic. It tied a knot in her chest, but it was not unpleasant.

It wasn't only the cheap thrill of nosing around in the Cullpeppers' bedroom that she was feeling. The Vicodin was kicking in. Her headache was gone and she felt giddy, a little bouncy, euphoric.

She bent down, chewing on a bite of donut, and pulled out the bottom drawer of Nancy's dresser. She stopped chewing as she stared down at the drawer's contents. She stayed like that for a while, bent forward at the waist, right hand on the drawer's handle, left holding the donut. She was not sure, at first, what she was seeing. A lot of black coils of something, silver studs.

It was leather. There was a black leather mask with two eye holes and a zipper over the mouth and silver studs along the seams. A whip was coiled up in the drawer. It was not a regular whip but had several strands. She had to think a moment to remember what that kind of whip was called. Some kind of tail ... cat tail?

"Cat o' nine tails," she muttered to herself.

A red ball gag was nestled in the center of the whip's coil. Beneath the whip, she saw silver handcuffs. Lying at the back of the drawer was a veiny, flesh-colored dildo.

Darlene tried to imagine Nancy and Harold using the equipment, and it made her laugh. Never in a million years would she have guessed. They just didn't seem to be the type. They were always so busy with social functions, charity events. They never even told dirty jokes. She wondered if they still used it, or if it stayed there in the bottom drawer, tucked away and neglected.

She tried to remember the last time she and Nancy had discussed their sex lives. It had been a long while. That usually meant things were good, because if they weren't, they complained. She had known Nancy for nearly fifteen years, ever since the Cullpeppers had moved into the house across the street, and they talked about everything with each other. But Nancy had never mentioned handcuffs or whips or leather masks.

Darlene closed the drawer and finished her donut as she went to Harold's dresser. The top drawer contained underwear and socks. Sweaters in the second drawer. Sweats and more socks in the third. She pulled out the bottom drawer. Just some old slippers. Nothing interesting or naughty.

Darlene went back to Nancy's dresser and opened the drawer that contained the boxes. She had opened two, but there were two more. She took one out and opened it. More pictures of Nancy and Harold together, but these were more explicit. They weren't simply fondling and playing. There was something harsh and ugly about the pictures, and Darlene shuffled through them quickly. She did not care to linger on them.

She put them back in their box, returned it to the drawer, and took out the fourth box. She opened it and found another stack of Polaroid snapshots. She took them out, and when she looked at the first one, her mouth slowly opened and her eyes gradually narrowed as she absorbed what she was seeing. She stumbled backward and dropped into a sitting position on the foot of the bed next to Carmen. Startled, the cat got up and hopped off the bed, hurried out of the room. Some of the pictures slipped from Darlene's grasp and fell to the floor.

In the photograph, Nancy was lying naked on a double bed with a white bottom sheet and a single matching pillow and nothing more. Nancy lay on her side, propped up on her right elbow, beside another naked woman who lay on her back, a woman Darlene had never seen before. The other woman was middle-aged with long, brown, grey-streaked hair pooled around her head on the pillow. Her entire body was a uniform gray with a dull yellow hue, arms straight at her sides, legs straight and somewhat apart. Her lips were parted, eyes open and staring blankly upward. Her body was painfully thin. Her hip bones and ribs stood out sharply against her flesh. Stretch marks marred her flat belly. Her breasts were flat folds of skin. Her face held no expression other than its total *lack* of expression. It was immediately clear to Darlene—although her mind tried to reject it repeatedly because surely it could not be, surely it could not *be*—that the woman was dead. Nancy's left hand fondled the corpse's breast, her thumb touching the pale nipple.

In the next picture, Harold sat naked on the edge of the bed with the dead woman between him and Nancy. His left hand rested on the woman's pudendum and he smiled up at someone out of the frame, apparently speaking.

The next picture showed Harold mounting the woman as Nancy held one of her gray legs aside.

In another picture, Harold held the woman's leg up while Nancy scissored her legs between the woman's and pressed their vaginas together. There was a look of great pleasure on Nancy's face, a look that made Darlene's stomach turn.

There were more pictures. In some of them, either Harold or Nancy appeared to be looking at and talking to other people out of the frame. They were not alone.

The camera stayed close on the bed and provided no view of the room they were in, just a glimpse of a pale, tile floor and a wall with cheap wood paneling.

The dead woman's expression never changed.

Darlene picked up the photographs she'd dropped and looked at them. The same dead woman was in all the pictures, but none of the other people in the room got in front of the camera, only Nancy and Harold. She counted the photos—there were thirty-six. In these pictures, as in all the others, the camera's flash was reflected as pinpoints of red in Nancy's and Harold's eyes, giving them a slightly demonic appearance.

Darlene felt strange. The Vicodin had given her a pleasant, floaty feeling, but now she also felt nauseated. It was a strange nausea that started in her stomach and seemed to spread throughout her body. As she put the pictures back in the small cardboard box, her bones felt sick. She stood, bent down and put the box back in the drawer, closed it and stood up straight again.

Something rubbed against her calves and Darlene cried out as she threw herself forward and bumped into the dresser. Everything on top of it rattled. She looked down to see Maxie, the Siamese, looking up at her. The cat meowed, then wandered off.

Darlene had to get out of the house. She checked to make sure she had the key in her pocket, then hurried down the hall and out the front door.

When she got home, she went into the bathroom and vomited the donuts into the toilet.

* * *

Darlene could not remember the last time she and Ralph had eaten at the dining room table together, facing each other. They always ate in the living room with the television on, usually the news. They talked during the commercials, although tonight they said little. For dinner, they had a tossed salad, the chili that had been cooking in the crock pot all day, and cornbread, with a Sara Lee cherry cobbler for dessert. Ralph had been quiet since he'd gotten home. He'd been quiet a lot lately, wondering how much longer he would have his job.

She had gone through her day on automatic pilot, struggling to push from her mind the images of that dead, gray woman in the pictures with Nancy and Harold. She kept the television on all day with the volume turned up extra loud, something she did not normally do. Shortly before Ralph came home, with dinner on the stove, she'd hurried across the street to feed and water the cats and iguana again. She'd done it as quickly as possible and rushed back home.

During a commercial break, she said, "Honey, didn't Nancy and Harold once say they were friends with somebody who works over at the Hawley and Bryan funeral home?"

He thought about it a moment as he chewed his food and watched a beer commercial. He sat in his club chair with his dinner on a TV tray before him. "Yeah, I think so. Didn't they say they knew the Hawley boy? Well, he's not a boy anymore, but the son, I mean. He's running the place now, I think. His dad's in a rest home, if I'm not mistaken."

"Yes, I...I think that's what they said." She sat at the end of the couch, her plate on her lap. She'd taken one bite, but wasn't hungry. She kept moving the food around on the plate with her fork, but didn't eat.

"Why?" Ralph said.

"What?"

"Why did you ask about the funeral home guy?"

"Oh. Nothing, just...wondering."

The news came back on and they watched. But Darlene absorbed nothing the newscaster said. He could've been speaking gibberish and she wouldn't have noticed. Her mind was on the photographs.

During the next commercial break, she said, "Ralph, there's something I have to tell you."

"What?"

"Today...this morning...when I was over at Nancy's...you know, feeding the cats and the iguana...."

When she said nothing more for several seconds, Ralph said, "Yeah? What?"

"I...found something."

"What do you mean, you *found* something?"

"Well, I was kind of...looking around."

"Looking around? You were *snooping*?"

She tried to smile, but only moved her lips. "You could say that."

"Why would you do something like that? I mean, how would you like it if Nancy went snooping through *your* things?"

"But this is...different."

"I don't see how it's any different."

"I found these...pictures."

"Oh, god. *Personal* pictures? Pictures nobody else was meant to see, right?"

"But they were—"

He held up his hands, palms out. "I don't want to hear about them."

"Listen to me, these were pictures of—"

"Dammit, I said I don't want to *hear* about them! I *knew* you shouldn't have agreed to housesit for them. I had a feeling. I had a feeling something bad would come of it. What were you *thinking*, snooping around in their things?"

"Listen to me, honey, these pictures—it's really bothering me, and I need to—"

"I *said* I don't want to hear about them. I mean it. That's private stuff. Leave it alone. You had no business getting into their things, and I don't want you to bring me into it. It *should* bother you. You should be ashamed of yourself. You know better than that. What were you *thinking*?"

Tears stung Darlene's eyes. She thought again of the expression on Nancy's face as she scissored her legs between the dead woman's...the look of pleasure...the way Nancy's chin jutted sharply and her eyes rolled back into her head beneath half-closed lids... and she suddenly felt like throwing up again. She stood and took her dinner into the kitchen, lifted the lid on the garbage can, and scraped her food off the plate.

She went into the bathroom, closed and locked the door, sat down on the toilet and cried.

* * *

The next day, Darlene took care of the Cullpeppers' cats and lizard before going to work. It was difficult keeping her mind on her job all day because she knew they would be back when she got home. She would have to face Nancy. How could she? How could she behave as if things were the same, when they weren't and never would be again?

The drive home seemed to go on forever, and yet it was over far too soon.

Harold's burgundy Saturn, the car they'd driven to Medford, was in their driveway when Darlene got home. She went into the house and straight to her bedroom, where she took off her clothes and put on a pair of sweats. She wanted to get comfortable, although putting on the sweats did not help; she had not felt comfortable since finding the pictures the previous day.

She put a pot of water on the stove to make spaghetti, then started preparing the sauce. Ralph would be home in half an hour.

Normally, she would go across the street and welcome Nancy and Harold back, give them their key. But she could not do it.

The doorbell rang. Darlene heard the front door open.

"Yoo-hoo!" Nancy called. "Dar?"

Darlene froze in front of the stove. She could not move, held her breath in her lungs.

The front door closed. Footsteps came down the hall.

"You in here, Dar? It's me. I brought you something from Oregon."

Nancy came to the kitchen doorway and stopped. Darlene exhaled, forced herself to smile as she turned to her. "Hi," she said as she got a jar of Newman's Own spaghetti sauce from the cupboard. Her smile did not feel right on her face, and she knew it was not convincing. But it was the best she could do.

Nancy held a green-and-burgundy Roseville vase in one hand, her checkbook in the other. "We stopped by some shops on the way out of Oregon this morning, and I found this. I know how much you like Roseville." She offered it to Darlene, smiling.

Each movement Darlene made was a conscious effort: stepping forward, reaching out, taking the vase in her hands, maintaining her smile. She brushed Nancy's hand with her own and a sickening chill passed over her.

"Thank you," she said, and her voice broke. "It's very nice, it's beautiful, thank you."

"Is something wrong?" Nancy asked.

"I'm fine. How was your trip?" Darlene found that, even when she tried, she could not look Nancy in the eyes.

"It was okay, under the circumstances. Instead of a service, they held a wake for Aunt Eva, and everyone got roaring drunk. She would've approved." Nancy opened her checkbook. "Now, I want to pay you. I asked around and found out that the going rate is—"

"No," Darlene said.

"I told you, I insist on—"

"I said, no." Darlene put the vase on the counter. Her heart pounded so hard in her chest, she feared Nancy would be able to hear it. "I don't want money, the vase is more than enough, Nancy."

"But I really want to—"

"*No.*" Darlene snapped the word a little too loudly. She took a breath. "Really, I'm serious. No money."

"Are you sure nothing's wrong?"

"Fine, everything's fine."

"No, it's not. Are you and Ralph fighting?"

Darlene grabbed onto that like a drowning woman clutching a life preserver. "Yes, yes, that's it, we're fighting."

Nancy frowned, tilted her head to one side, and stepped toward Darlene.

Darlene immediately took two steps back.

"Honey, what's the matter?" Nancy said, frowning. "You're a mess."

"Don't worry about it. I'll be fine, really, just fine."

"Do you want to talk about—"

"No, I don't want to talk."

Nancy perked up a little, smiled. "I've got an idea. After dinner tonight, why don't you and Ralph come over for drinks. That sometimes helps when you're fighting, you know, to go to neutral ground and just—"

"No. Thank you. But no."

Nancy stepped forward again, spread her arms to hug Darlene. Darlene backed into the refrigerator.

As she embraced Darlene, Nancy said, "Well, something's got you upset, honey, you're as—"

"Don't touch me!" Darlene shouted, and pushed her away. Tears sprang to her eyes and she began to shake all over. "Please, just...stay away."

"What...I don't understand, why are you...what's *wrong*, Dar?"

Darlene put her right hand over her mouth as she sobbed. She stepped around Nancy, went to the round kitchen table and leaned on it heavily, left hand flat, elbow locked. She cried into her hand for a while as Nancy stared at her, open-mouthed and frowning. Finally, Darlene turned to her, looked at her without meeting her eyes.

She said, "I can't...I can't...I can't see you anymore. Please don't ask why, but I can't. I just can't. You can't come over anymore. I can't see you anymore. I just can't."

Slowly, Nancy's eyes grew larger. She raised her right hand slowly, put her palm to her cheek. "Oh, my god," she whispered. "What did you find?"

Darlene's shoulders hitched with more sobs. "I can't, Nancy. I just *can't*."

"Oh, my god."

"Pluh-please, don't say anything."

"You found the pictures."

"I'm sorry. I shouldn't have."

Nancy's face slackened. "You were poking around...in my things."

"I had no business. I shouldn't have. But...I did. I'm sorry."

"Oh, my god."

"Please go, Nancy."

"But you've got to understand. It was just a one-time thing. And she was homeless. She had no family, no one at all."

As Nancy spoke, Darlene put her hands over her ears and clenched her eyes shut. "I don't want to hear it!"

"What...what about Ralph?"

After a moment, Darlene lowered her hands and shook her head. "He doesn't know. I won't tell him. Just go. Please, just go."

Looking stunned, Nancy slowly turned and left the kitchen.

Darlene listened to her footsteps down the hall, heard the front door open, then close. She took a paper towel from the roll and dabbed at her eyes. She did not want Ralph to find her this way. She went to the sink and splashed cold water on her face, got another paper towel and dried herself. She took a few deep breaths.

Even if she never saw Nancy again, she knew she'd never be able to forget the pictures, no matter how hard she tried.

* * *

"Wanna go over and see Harold and Nancy this evening?" Ralph said. "Maybe have a drink or two? Harold hasn't said two words since they've been back."

Four days had passed. Darlene had heard nothing from Nancy, had not even seen her across the street.

"Not tonight," Darlene said. "I have a headache."

"You should take something for it."

"We're out of aspirin. All we've got is Tylenol, and that never helps me."

"Maybe Nancy has something. You should give her a call."

"I'll just run down to the market and get some aspirin. We need some anyway."

"Okay, if you say so."

* * *

One week later, Darlene came home from work to find a sign in front of the Cullpeppers' house that read 'FOR SALE,' with the realtor's logo and phone number below.

She parked the car in the driveway, went into the house, sat on the edge of the bed and cried.

ABOUT THE AUTHOR
RAY GARTON

Ray Garton has been nominated for the Bram Stoker Award and is the author of more than sixty novels, novellas, short story collections, movie novelizations and TV tie-ins. His exceptional portfolio of work spans the genres of horror, crime and suspense.

Garton's 1987 erotic vampire novel *Live Girls* was called "artful" by the *New York Times* and was nominated for the Bram Stoker Award. In 2006, he received the Grand Master of Horror Award at the World Horror Convention in San Francisco. His 2001 comedy thriller *Sex and Violence in Hollywood* is being developed for the screen.

His most recent novels, *Trailer Park Noir* and *Meds* (a thriller with deadly side effects), are available in paperback and as ebooks from E-Reads. And his seventh collection, *Wailing and Gnashing of Teeth*, was recently published by Cemetery Dance Publications. His short story "Second Opinion" appears in *Dark Visions: A Collection of Modern Horror - Volume One* from Grey Matter Press.

Garton lives in northern California with his wife Dawn.

EMPTY
A.A. GARRISON

Shit and Cunt were husband and wife, named after famous saints. As ordained by a holy book, which all agreed upon, the two raised children to be sold into slavery. Cunt was some months pregnant with their latest offering. Their child-farm was just out-side the Dying City, in a waste of used-up catheters.

The two were in the barn, slopping the kids, when Shit went empty.

He dropped his slop bucket and stood up straight, stressing his suit of stitched human skin.

"Disaster," he said.

"There is no God," he said.

"All is forsaken," he said.

In response, Cunt checked the little gauge in Shit's head. Sure enough, the needle was on '*E.*'

"Wait here," she told Shit, after finishing with the slop and laying down fresh sawdust. "I'll get the prophet."

"No God," he said, staring. "Disaster."

Cunt left him in the stall, taking the slop bucket with her.

* * *

The prophet resided in the Dying City. It didn't take long to hitch a ride.

Cunt stood at the roadside, raising her maternity dress to each passing vehicle. Several stopped to snap pictures—Cunt had distinctive genitals—but no takers. Not until the truck.

Clanky and obscene, the truck had been repurposed into a stagecoach and powered by men on treadmills who chased dangling carrots. The slaves' treadmilling was furious, yet the driver still whipped at them occasionally for something to do.

The truck pulled alongside the blonde with the interesting clit-jewelry, the driver tugging at the reins and saying, "Whoa! Whoa!" The treadmilling stopped.

Cunt lowered her human-skin dress. Dust settled. The treadmill slaves raptly stared at the carrots, slobbering in their collective trance.

"The City?" the driver asked her, in greeting.

"The City," Cunt said.

"Well hop on up." He patted the bench with one hand and undid his codpiece with the other. "I'm goin' there for some new carrots, and maybe new slaves, if I get hungry enough on the way."

The present carrots were moldering and foul, with no orange left on them.

Cunt mounted the coach heavily, holding her merchandise-swollen belly. She put the slop bucket beside her on the seat, then raised her dress again, as was moral and upright.

"Heeya!" the driver said as he mounted her, multitasking. The slaves resumed their treading. The truck's tires groaned.

* * *

The Dying City steepled the horizon, building itself as it grew closer. Past a gate skewered with decorative heads, bloody streets offered splendor, bustling in a sleepless furor of drugs and need. Buoyant vendors quoted reasonable prices for living wares. Secretive shops lay in tentative states, stocked with all manner of human-origin goods. Wide-eyed citizens conspired in any dark place, courting Illusion and its deathly brethren.

"I'll infect you yet!" pledged a festering, one-eyed knave. Violence. Consumption. A dervish of snarling ruin. The masters might eat you before the dogs.

The truck stopped in a restless market square, its tires bumping over bodies and cast-off flesh.

Cunt drank it in, at home here. She uncoupled from the driver and jumped down, taking the slop bucket with her. The two exchanged lewd gestures, as was customary, and the driver re-started the slaves.

"Farewell, lass!" he called, waving a hat of cured scrotums. Then: "Heeya! Heeya!"

At once, Cunt armed herself with razor, shiv and inserts over her teeth to enhance biting. Her special panties were booby-trapped with broken glass that made clinking noises like snow falling on windows.

Thus fortified, she set off for the prophet.

Through the fetid market she walked, past huts selling people-sausage, down streets where bodily fluids accumulated. She was attacked; she defended herself; she licked away blood. Looting her slain enemies proved unprofitable. In her wake, skinners made quick work of the corpses, in the way of ants—to the tannery!

The prophet was where Cunt had expected him to be, in an open grotto along Castration Street. The ageless man wore a hair shirt and hair pants and a hair hat, his mangy epidermis ornamented with keepsakes and foreskins. His shoes were fashioned from God's holy word, and were periodically read from. He carried a staff of anonymous bone twined with heathen sinew, to be waved with authority—hoorah!

The prophet quoted scripture in no specific format:

"God hath not sorrow, for He dines on small children! Rape is love! Resistance is wickedness!"

Amidst a sort of dance, the prophet prophesied, announced profundities and explained God's intent. His towering stage commanded respect and defeated dispute by height alone. A crowd fawned over him always, swaying and agreeing and concocting praises. Out of the way, a scribe recorded these events—so shall it be written.

Cunt joined the crowd, holding her slop bucket and a shiv still dripping. No one noticed her arrival, their faces blank and enamored, too faithful to be aware. Every so often, one of them would shout an acclamation, or enter holy hysterics. At the prophet's request, there might be music or suicide.

"Destruction is worship! Allow Him control! Praise almighty Fuck God!"

The sermon was long and compelling and paused only for sexual intercourse with select attendees. When the prophet urinated, a disciple waited with a genuine gold chalice, soon topped with hot, popping foam. The recipient then made off with this treasure, to be preserved and cherished.

"Surrender to Him your words and fluids! The heretic resists His love!"

In finale, a collection was taken, the prophet passing around his flimsy hair hat. It soon brimmed with tribute of drugs and flesh and sharp, sharp knives. When it came Cunt's way, something in it was moving.

Just after the service, as the new dead were swept away, a voice raised from nearby, stealing the crowd's attention.

"*Seek reality!*" it called, without demand. "*Lay down your illusions! There is hope!*" It was another prophet, but of some perverse doctrine. He carried a sign that echoed his words.

He approached the assembly of bleeding and drooling people, who regarded him warily. "*Seek reality and be free, friends,*" the pervert pled. "*We here are pathologically unable to acknowledge reality. Surrender all preconception, all assumption, all clinging. Only then shall we find reality and its abundance. Empty your cup so it may be filled.*"

It took some seconds for the crowd to decide on this creature. They looked to their prophet for permission, and it was granted.

With a grotesque grace, God's children fell upon the heathen interloper, reducing him to featureless meat. During the melee, a man came away with an arm; a child, the blasphemous head. They cooked the false prophet over a fire, using his sign as a spit. The true prophet blessed the feast, and all agreed that God smiled on this.

* * *

It took hours for the crowd to disperse, but Cunt was patient. She ate ribs from the false prophet while waiting, and they were good. Her baby kicked with each bite, surely in praise.

The true prophet had retired to the same stage from which he'd preached, seated amidst nude and supplicant women on short leashes. When Cunt approached, he looked up and said, "State your business, beautiful one."

"It's my husband," she said. "He's empty."

"Empty, eh?" The prophet stood from his lordly throne and descended the stage. Up close and at eye level he didn't seem so special.

Cunt held out her slop bucket to him, hoping to have it filled, but it went ignored.

"What's your name, child?" the prophet asked through bloody teeth.

Cunt said her name.

"Ah, like the Hallowed Saint of Menses."

Cunt nodded patiently. People had been making this comparison her whole life.

"God requires payment, first, Cunt," the prophet said. He looked her up and down. "Doest thou wish to render payment?"

Cunt said, "Well, I guess." The other prophets had never asked for payment. *But what are you gonna do?*

The prophet dug in his hair shirt and pulled out a high-tech device. He pointed it and pushed a button. A glowing portal opened in midair, lighting the immediate area. On the other side, a sunlit cityscape awaited.

Cunt looked on, unimpressed. *The prophets and their portals...*

"Do this unto almighty Fuck God, and thy bucket shalt be filled," the prophet offered. He then handed over instructions on parchment of cured human skin, followed by a gun and a serrated knife.

Cunt read the note, then said, "Okay. Be right back."

When she hopped through the portal, the prophet was back to dancing.

* * *

The portal was a wormhole leading back in time to a place called America—the Dying City's precursor. Here, people pretended they weren't predatory, which would eventually give way to the outright predation in the modern-day City.

Cunt was to slay an American demon, according to the prophet's instructions. She reread this and said, "Okay."

The demon's name was A.A. Garrison, an enemy of God and a writer of blasphemous literature. The note provided an address, urged Cunt to aim for the head or the heart and to use the gun's entire clip. She cocked a round and holstered the gun in her maternity skin-dress. The knife went with the rest of her blades, secreted on her person.

The portal opened into a cozy, little alleyway where no one saw her arrive. Then Cunt made her way through the American wastes. The people here were, sacrilegiously, wearing cloth and animal leathers rather than the cured skins of their enemies, unlike any right-thinking child of God. This made Cunt wince with disgust.

On her way to the demon's lair, Cunt was thinking how she loved God, and her husband Shit, and the prophet, and the City. Then she heard a voice.

"*That's not love,*" it said faintly, from her right.

Cunt wheeled around and a ghost hovered nearby. She at once recognized it as the last false prophet she'd helped kill and eat—as opposed to the one of the week before.

"What do you want?" she asked, neutrally.

"*You were thinking of love, but that's not love.*"

"Oh?" she asked, eyebrows raised. It certainly felt like love.

"*We live in a carnivorous society, but have reached a consensus that we don't,*" the ghost of the "prophet" explained to Cunt. "*We prey on one another, physically and emotionally, and then reach a consensus that this is normal—that it is inevitable. So we believe in our exploitation, call it love, and we never know better because of this consensus and its skewed perceptions. Such is consensus reality.*"

"You say 'consensus' a lot," was Cunt's rebuttal. It sounded good, so she believed it fully. She put in some earplugs kept especially for jerks like this and went on her way.

"*There's hope!*" the ghost called after her. "*Consensus only has power over you if you subscribe to it...!*" He trailed off as Cunt got distance. Ghosts were slow.

Nearing her destination, in a cheery little block of buildings, Cunt heard murmuring. Then, when she pulled out her earplugs, the murmuring became shouting. A crowd was amassed around A.A. Garrison's home, as if it were a prophet.

The protesters were lined ten deep on the lawn, the driveway and the doorstep. Signs pumped from the mass, these reading 'UNAMERICAN,' or 'LOVE IT OR LEAVE IT' or 'TOO MANY ADVERBS.' One of them, a red-faced woman, used a bullhorn to reassure her colleagues and quote verses.

Cunt scanned the faces, and they looked as bloodthirsty as any-one in the Dying City.

Apparently, they thought this Garrison a demon too.

"Turn or burn!" cried the bullhorn.

The protesters: "Turn or burn! Turn or burn! Turn or burn!"

The chanting continued as Cunt pushed her way to the back of the house. She looked through the windows—none of which displayed the organs of God-haters as demanded by Menshakiah 10:11—and the downstairs was empty. The back door was un-locked.

Cunt found the demon seated quietly on the floor in an upstairs bedroom. It was disguised as a man of no particular description. Beside him lay an open notebook of writing, surely blasphemous and perverse. His eyes were closed and he was breathing rhythmi-cally, in meditation against the noisy protest.

"Hey, demon," Cunt said, making Garrison open his eyes.

He looked her over, with recognition. "But I didn't write it this way!" he cried, upon seeing the gun. Then it fired, hitting him square between the eyes. His blood covered his papers, blotting out his lies.

Cunt was good at sawing off heads, so it took only minutes to liberate Garrison's. His hair was long—like all demons'—so the head was easy to carry. Having forgotten the protest, she unlocked the front door and went outside.

The shouting silenced at once, the signs flagging. The crowd studied the blood-caked woman before them, deciding where her sympathies lie. Then, upon seeing the severed head of their sworn enemy, the people became excited all over again. Their signs returned to their pivoting.

"The beast is dead!" the bullhorn cheered.

The crowd: "The beast is dead! The beast is dead! The beast is dead!"

In a sudden wind, Cunt was swept up on hands and shoulders. She was paraded through the crowd like a hero wearing laurels, the demon's head swinging every which way.

"The beast is dead! The beast is dead!"

The chanting kept on as Cunt kicked down the hands and shoved herself away from the glassy-eyed crowd. Several stared intently at the head, and she growled them off. One got grabby and she used her shiv. The bullhorn was still at it when Cunt left the neighborhood.

Back in town, she received ghastly stares from the Americans, as if they'd never seen a severed head. She found the alley of her arrival, and the portal was as she'd left it.

* * *

The prophet received A.A. Garrison's head with outstretched hands. He inspected it for some time, turning it around and around.

"He had only one head, yes?" the prophet asked Cunt.

"Only one," she confirmed. She picked up the slop bucket in expectation.

The prophet dropped the head and kicked it to a nearby pile with a weary sigh. "Ah well. I thought killing him might end all this. He wrote us, you know." He indicated the world.

Cunt nodded politely. She extended the slop bucket a little, involuntarily.

The prophet noticed it. "Oh," he said distractedly. "That's right. Your husband."

Cunt nodded again, somewhat eagerly.

With some gurgling noises, the prophet leaned forward and vomited the bucket full. After some dry heaves, he finned his hands and blessed the fuel.

Cunt smiled genuinely. "Thank you, prophet," she said. "Thanks."

"God's bounty upon you!" he said as Cunt started away, her slop bucket sloshing.

Back at the road, she once more raised her skin-dress.

* * *

Shit remained in their barn, unmoved in the slightest. The crotch of his pants was wet, and he was sobbing. The kids squirmed around his feet.

"There is no God," he was still gibbering. "Disaster."

Wordlessly, Cunt reached for his head and rummaged through his hair, feeling for the fuel hatch. With a click, she opened it up and fit a funnel inside.

A healthy glugging as the prophet's vomit poured home.

For some seconds, Shit stayed in his broken state, his face contorted with godlessness. Then his cheek twitched and his eyes filled up, his forehead smoothing.

"Destruction is worship!" he proclaimed, making the children look. "Rape is love! God hath not sorrow, for He dines on small children!"

He took Cunt in his arms and kissed her into a swoon. His erection said his faith had returned.

"Destruction is worship! Praise almighty Fuck God!"

ABOUT THE AUTHOR
A.A. GARRISON

A.A. Garrison is a thirty-year-old man living in the mountains of North Carolina, USA, where he writes and landscapes comfortably above sea level.

His short fiction has appeared in dozens of magazines, anthologies and web journals, as well as the Pseudopod webcast. He is the author of the campy, post-apocalyptic horror novel, *The End of Jack Cruz,* published by Montag Press.

His short story, "Variations on Soullessness," will be published in the upcoming collection *Dark Visions: A Collection of Modern Horror - Volume Two* from Grey Matter Press.

DIS

MICHELE GARBER

The demon has taken control again. I can see it in her eyes, the stagnant muddy-brownness sucking at me as she speaks, like wading through mental shit.

"Nothing to say? That's right; you like to watch, don't you?" Her legs part ever so slightly, enough to taunt me but too little to justify a response, to call attention to her behavior.

I ignore her and ask for Karen again.

"Aw, poor Dr. Weiss. Such a hard cock and nowhere to put it. Am I making you uncomfortable?" This time her thighs spread wide enough for me to see the entire show, the engorged, pink labial folds not quite hiding the glistening wetness deeper within.

I'm struggling and hoping she doesn't see it.

I need to consult with Roger soon.

She looks at my impassive face and grins, a slow spread of satisfied delight that accompanies the languid close of her legs under the short denim skirt. "Karen's here, Doc. She knows how much you want..." A gentle pulse of the knees outward for emphasis. "...her. To come forward, I mean. See you soon." Her body goes limp for a moment, her head a drooping flower dying for water, and then she's back again. She blanches, seeing my face. "Dr. Weiss? Was it her again?"

I tell her yes. My legs are crossed to hide things.

Karen starts to weep. And I find myself horrified, not because I'm enjoying it, but because I'm not horrified at all.

* * *

There's silence on the line, and I imagine Roger digesting what I've told him. "What's going on, Tony? In all the time I've known you, I've never seen you deliberately ignore what a dissociative client's telling you, especially an alter. What's making you retreat from working with this particular aspect of Karen's case?"

I tell Roger how intractable Karen is, how self-destructive, how overtly sexual. I say nothing about myself.

"None of that ever stopped you before." He hesitates for a moment, then asks, "How's Trina doing?"

The phone is slippery in my hands, slick with sweat. I make my excuses and terminate the conversation, promising to call him back tomorrow.

I have no intention of doing that.

The building is deserted. Everyone else has gone home. I spend a few minutes in the bathroom, which is all it takes, and howl with the release, then in anguish, because the delicate, pink flower of Karen's cunt is all I can see.

* * *

Ani is there when I get home. "Daddy!" she screams, flinging herself into my arms. "Guess what I did at school today? Guess!"

"Elephants," I say. "You rode elephants."

"No, silly Daddy, I drew you a picture. Look!" Ani wriggles away from me and snatches a piece of paper off the wide, oak kitchen table, thrusting it toward my face. "See? Here's me, and you, and Mommy." She points first to two crayon-scrawled stick figures standing outside a house and then one sitting in a wheelchair, a green oxygen tank hooked up to its throat. They are all smiling.

I tell her it's lovely, kiss her and ask her to go help Jennifer. I can smell fennel and other savory aromas emanating from the kitchen, and my stomach growls as my daughter skips away happily. I wish I could be like her, ignorant of any other way of life.

I might even be happy again.

"Ten minutes," Jennifer says when I walk into the kitchen, and I inform the frizzy, chocolate-blonde back of her head where I'm going. I walk across the hall to the great room, wincing at the TV's volume, and bend down to kiss Trina's cheek.

"You're home late." Terse and sulky. I tense up, moving away from her chair.

Please, not tonight. Not again.

"Paperwork." I fling the excuse out and hope she'll gobble it down unquestioningly, chum for her suspicious shark mind.

Her eyes jab at me. "Really? That's the best you can come up with?"

Trina is judge, jury and executioner. All three roles fill her with black, vicious delight. My guilt pins me down, forcing me to allow her whatever nasty pleasures she can still experience.

So I say nothing.

"Why, Tony, I do believe I've rendered you speechless." The grin is familiar, and my heart stutters a bit until my rational mind takes over. "Don't you want me anymore?" Her voice is sultry, challenging me to respond.

I respond automatically, telling her that of course I still want her and love her very much. It sounds mechanical, even to my ears.

"Mmmm. As much as you want Karen and her juicy little pussy? You were enjoying that today, weren't you, Tony?" Her whisper sounds like a hiss in the quiet room, the serpent striking lightning-fast to fill my veins with poison almost before I can notice. My heart pounds painfully, and my first thoughts are: *How the hell could she know, that's not possible, I never told her about Karen and how does she know what's in my head, in my fucking head?* But I say something else altogether.

"Shut up, Trina. Ani might hear you."

"Hear what, Tony? About how much you wanted to get down on your knees today in your dignified psychologist's suit and eat one of your clients out until she begged you to let her come, dreamed about clamping a hand over her mouth so the receptionist and other clients wouldn't hear, flipping her over onto your desk and fucking her sweet little ass as your hands started to choke the air out of her like her daddy's did so many years ago?"

Salacious. Trina's eyes watch me tremble with rage and terror, drinking my distress like liquid candy. The demon is here, now, sitting fraily in a wheelchair, daring me to lash out.

I don't believe in demons.

The world goes dark for a moment, and I hear Trina's voice take on a note of concern.

"Tony? Are you okay?" Vision returns and only my wife remains, her wan, pale features swimming back into focus. The familiar face that I fell in love with so many years ago.

"Yes, I'm okay."

Trina nods uncertainly, then blows into the plastic tube near her mouth to get the wheelchair moving, rolling across the hall into the kitchen. I hear her talking with Jennifer and wonder numbly if I'm going crazy. If I weren't so shaken, I might actually try to diagnose myself.

Instead, I join my family for dinner and try to forget what just happened, try to tell myself everything will be all right, hoping this time I might actually believe my own lies.

* * *

Sleep comes easily for me. Even over the last few years, I've had no trouble slipping into unconsciousness. Perhaps I use up all my guilt during the day.

But there are dreams. Every night, without exception, I return across the charnel bridge and plunge into the city's chthonic depths. I tell myself I have no choice, that the horrors are self-punishment inflicted until I forgive myself, but my steps quicken as I descend the last few yards of the great arch. The fiends at the Gate allow me entrance, knowing smirks and leering glances slithering over my body, a physical insult to my dreaming mind.

And She's there. Waiting for me, flail in hand. "Welcome back, Tony. I had fun today, didn't you?" The leathery tail flicks back and forth, scraping across the twisted stones.

Yes. Fun. Why Trina?

Her tail twitches once and goes still. "Why Trina?" she repeats, the suppurating brow furrowing and relaxing in quick succession. "Well, isn't it obvious?"

If it were obvious, I wouldn't ask.

She laughs the harsh bark of an ancient bawd. "Get down on your knees and I'll explain it to you."

I obey, hoping for answers and pain-tinged pleasure.

"Lick," she commands, and the scaly legs part, waiting.

I know dreams can be controlled, can be molded. I know this.

The acid burns my tongue, and I close my eyes, not wanting to see the damage. I know the pain is only real in the dream. "Yes," she coos, "you deserve this, don't you?" My lips are dissolving into a bloody, meaty mush, my teeth exposed, and I swallow, the acid searing my throat and stomach. Vomit gushes from me in a noisome rush, spilling food and crimson chunks of my own guts before me. I collapse onto a floor black from the release of others' bowels, gobbets of their flesh and lifeblood, and I writhe in agony.

"I said lick." And I do.

All of it.

"Such a pretty face," she says, taking what's left of my chin in one clawed hand and turning it from side to side. "It suits you. Again." The blackened stump of my tongue, cracked and oozing, dutifully pokes out again and resumes its work as the pain makes this hideous world distant, then unreachable as I fall into the void.

* * *

"God!" she cries softly from above me, writhing.

My chin is wet and slick and I don't know where I am.

"Why didn't we do this before?" She pants as I crawl away and fumble for the lights, the glare blinding after so much dark.

The mirror. My familiar face stares back, the lips intact, the skin whole. But I'm not alone—I see Jennifer in the bed, one arm flung over her own face to shut out the light.

"What have I done?"

Jennifer sighs. "Tony, you've got to let the guilt go. You're not a saint." She lies back, letting the pillows cradle her, and the grin surfaces. Her grin. "I'll second that. Nice tongue. Too bad your wife can't feel it anymore."

"Shut. Up."

"What did you say?" The mirror-Jennifer looks frightened, and angry. "I thought you wanted this. I thought it might help." She swallows, her tawny features working. "I know I shouldn't love you."

"Not you. Her."

Jennifer's eyes are wary. "I don't understand you, Tony. Who are you talking about?"

"Never mind. You should go now."

She slides from my solitary bed, trying for dignity, and I see her breasts swinging pendulously as she stumbles around the bedroom, gathering her clothes from floor and chair and dresser. She brushes past me, clutching the bundle to her like a shield and trying not to look at me.

"I'm sorry. It's my fault."

Her chin comes up. "Yes, it is, Tony. All of it." And she's gone, retreating to her room down the hall.

I wish I knew who spoke at the end.

For the first time in two years, I cannot sleep.

* * *

I'm doing okay at work today, though I'm exhausted by mid-afternoon. Roger has called twice already, and both times I instruct my receptionist to inform him that I'm unavailable. Carla sounds uncomfortable, but does what I ask. If only everything was so simple.

Gigi is my last client before the weekend, and I'm grateful to end on a high note. The intelligent ones with moderate insight are generally easy, even when they're as withdrawn and depressed as Gigi usually is. Her thick, black braids make her look far younger than she is, a pubescent teenager taking a demure seat on the couch across from me.

Next to me.

I see a mix of fear and want warring in her uncertain gaze, inches from my own. The braids are gone, her obsidian hair loose and flowing in a glossy stream over her thin shoulders. "Is this better, Dr. Weiss?" My hand hangs in mid-air, fingers inches from touching her.

Wait, what—

"Oh, Dr. Weiss! What beautiful eyes you have. Now you say,

'The better to lust with.'" Her narrowed eyes watch with clinical detachment, gauging my reaction.

I can't seem to move.

She sighs, impatient. "You really are slow, aren't you, Tony?" My client's body folds its legs underneath itself and starts to unbutton the prim, white cotton blouse, baring small, high breasts and golden skin.

There are no such things as demons.

"Stop it...please stop...it hurts!" The screaming is high and piteous, deafening in my left ear. There's a coppery taste in my mouth, something rolling around inside it. I spit into my hand and find the pink eraser-stump of a nipple floating in a puddle of viscous bright red fluid. I gag, realizing that Gigi is pinned beneath me, her face a rictus of terror and betrayal. I pull out of her and sit up, unable to tear my eyes from that tiny nubbin of tender flesh.

Oh my God.

"He's not here, Tony. Not for what you just did." She's up and crawling toward me over the cushions, blood pouring from her savaged breast. "How about two for two? A matched set?" The vulnerable dusky-rose nippleblossom hovers before my sticky mouth, waiting. "C'mon, there's a good boy. I know how much you enjoy this." It traces a path over my upper lip, daring me to respond.

It's you. But you're not real.

"I'm not? Then you must be doing all this, Tony. Isn't that right?"

No. I couldn't do something like this.

"Really? What about last night?" She's sitting back on her haunches, staring at me curiously as one hand fingers the open wound on her chest, an obscene masturbatory display.

That's different. Jennifer wanted that.

"No, Tony. In the city. In Dis. You and me." Her fingers stop moving. "You haven't forgotten, have you?" The dark eyes gleam with fury at the thought.

No. I remember.

She preens, but the rage never leaves her. "I knew you wouldn't. Let me give you a little present, Tony. We'll clean up the mess together." She leans in close and starts to whisper in my ear, the words burrowing into my brain and nesting securely in the nourishing pink jellyfolds.

Suddenly, everything makes sense again.

* * *

I'm standing at the front door of my own house. In a moment I will go inside, but right now I'm remembering when this was a home. Before the affair, before the accident. Long before Her.

I have another home now.

I hear a roaring sound as my key turns in the lock, and the door swings inward. It's the rush of a dark river carrying me forward and away from the miserable swamp of my life, the beat of dirty, mottled wings, the maelstrom of dissolution.

"Daddy!" Ani runs toward me down the hall, slowing to a walk and then stopping as she sees my face. "Daddy?" She knows in the way all children know.

I step over the threshold, letting the door shut gently, and enter another world.

* * *

June 24, 2013

Dear Ginny,

I hope this letter finds you well, my friend. As I'm sure you noted by the postmark, I'm writing from the sunny shores of Florida. A nice place to spend one's retirement, or so I've been told.

Although I've sold the practice, I still keep up with news in our profession. When I heard through the grapevine you would be treating Tony, I was relieved. He needs someone good, someone who can retain some sort of objectivity and see him for the good man he once was, who loved his family and his work. It's too easy to demonize what we don't understand, and I hope that this information sheds some light on the events that occurred before and during his psychotic episode.

I believe the majority of the trouble began after Trina's accident, which resulted in her quadriplegia. Some marriages become strained after the birth of a child, when it is no longer "we two" and attention to the primary relationship flags. Tony strayed, plain and simple, and confessed the lapse to Trina. She was hurt and angry, of course, and although no one wants to place blame, a combination of reckless driving and slick roads apparently caused the accident. Trina lost control of the van, hitting a tree and breaking her neck.

After Trina left the hospital, Tony hired Jennifer Meyer as her care attendant. The arrangement seemed to be working fairly well, although Trina was understandably bitter. I can only imagine how much grief, regret and guilt Tony's had to shoulder along the way. I know he went to therapy for a while, but terminated treatment prematurely, in my opinion. I tried to confront him several times without success. I wish to God I'd tried harder.

That night I stopped by his house, thinking we might chat a bit more about the case he was struggling with. No one answered after I rang the doorbell several times, although I could see lights on all over the house. I tried the door, found it unlocked, and went inside.

You'll have to forgive me if I wax a bit matter-of-fact here, as I still have difficulty remembering.

The upper half of someone's body was lying sprawled in the hallway, a cast iron skillet overturned next to them. Looking back on it now, I can't believe how long it took me to act. I was busy, you see, trying to figure out why there was this sense of wrongness somehow, like looking at one of those Magic Eye puzzles and knowing something should be there but you're not seeing it. Then it clicked and I was fighting not to vomit.

The head was completely flat. Pounded so with the skillet, which was covered with fragments of white skull, brain matter and blondish-brown hair. Her lower garments had been removed and a chef's knife protruded from between her legs. Deep bite marks covered almost every inch of exposed skin.

I didn't call the police at that point. I probably should have, because that would have been sensible, and I'm not a strong young man anymore. I think common sense had been shocked out of me by that point.

I went to Trina's room next, fearing the worst. Totally helpless as she was, my next concern was for her.

This is harder than I thought it would be.

Her limbs had been completely disarticulated, scattered across the wide hospital bed and over the usually clean hardwood floor. Several fingers had been stuffed into her vagina, toes in her mouth. I saw her wedding ring winking at me, sparkling in the overhead light, and felt my mind trying to tear free of its moorings. I chose to vomit instead, adding my own bile and half-digested food to the pools of congealed blood soaking nearly everything in the room. Her eyes stared up at the ceiling, unblinking, and I knew she was gone, had been for a while. I believe she died from exsanguination, the femoral arteries severed crudely with a handsaw and pumping the blood from her quickly, as the adrenaline of terror hastened the process.

I hope you can forgive the blotches on the page, here. As you well know, the curse and blessing of a good psychologist is empathy.

As I stood over Trina, I heard muttering coming from the living room. I did have enough presence of mind left to call the police on my cell phone and give basic information about what had happened. They advised me to get out of the house and I said okay. They could've said anything and I would've agreed. I wasn't processing any of it. And there was Ani to think of.

But I still wish I had left, even so. I'd never have the next image burned indelibly into my mind.

Passing through the kitchen, I removed a knife from the wooden block, telling myself I should get out; I might get both Ani and myself killed if the perpetrator became agitated by my presence. But how could I leave a five-year-old alone with a sociopath and murderer? I couldn't do it.

And God help me, I stepped into the living room.

I'd found Ani and the intruder. He was hunched over her small form, lying limp on the coffee table, and doing something to her. I called out sharply for him to get away from her, to leave her alone. He straightened and turned around, giving me a clear view of the entire scene.

I dropped the knife, shock severing the connection between my brain and hand as abruptly as if the nerves had been cut. It was Tony. Naked and bleeding from the ragged stump of what had once been his penis.

"Hi, Roger," he had said. "You here to help?"

And he grinned. The most terrible thing I've ever seen was that smile, totally devoid of all sanity and good.

I couldn't respond to that. All I could do was see, you understand? Witness the full scope of the evil present in that room. There was nothing I could do for the child— her soul had mercifully vacated the broken shell of her earthly body, taken wing and flown away. I can only hope that whatever remains of her doesn't remember any part of her death. Surely the universe isn't so cruel?

I could see that it was his own severed member that Tony had been jamming into her fragile body over and over, aided by the end of a wooden spoon threaded through the urethra to give it rigidity. Postmortem, I suspect, because Ani had already been smothered with feces, choking on what had been shoved into her mouth and nasal cavity.

"I had to do it, Roger," Tony explained, resuming the horrible in-and-out motion. "She was in them. Don't you see?"

I could hear sirens in the distance. They sounded like screams.

I want to believe that some vestige of the kind, compassionate man I once knew survives, but that sort of belief is harder to come by these days. If anyone can help Tony find his way back, it's you. That much I do know.

Give me a call when you can. Until then, take care and good luck.

Roger

P.S. There's one more thing I should tell you, the last thing he said to me before the police led him away, howling and struggling in their grasp in order to return and finish his terrible work. A single sentence that encompasses the horror of that night, and has haunted me ever since: "This is how we do things in Dis."

ABOUT THE AUTHOR
MICHELE GARBER

Michele Garber was born and raised in northern Indiana, which should in no way be held accountable for how she turned out.

After narrowly escaping a doctorate in psychology, Garber embarked upon a heroic quest to use her arcane knowledge of the human psyche to terrify, tempt and titillate readers. Her first published short story, "Tequila Sunset," appeared in the Northern Frights Publishing anthology *War of the Worlds: Frontlines*. Her work will also be featured in Columbia Art League's interdisciplinary exhibit, *Interpretations*, in the fall of 2013.

Michele now lives on the outskirts of St. Louis, Missouri, with her family and enjoys reading, prestidigitation and making extreme cakes in her spare time.

DWELLERS
PAUL M. COLLRIN

Out in the heart of the desert's darkness, yellow snakes of light lit black tar and broken white lines were turned to blurs by speed. Neither of the car's occupants paid attention to the road they traveled. It was one they both knew well. There was no need to look for landmarks—in the desert there were none. Night here was black... and nothing else.

"Jesus, Richmond, couldn't we meet the Freak somewhere else?" Scrye didn't like the desert, didn't trust it. Out here in the middle of nowhere was where they came to push Richmond's synthetic miracles.

Richmond said nothing, only watching the road. Scrye could almost guess what he was thinking. No matter where they went, it would be the same—the walking living dead shambling in listless shuffles. Pock-marked arms screaming for puncture, seeping no blood, only a thin, viscous, yellow trickle of infection—veins that pumped death instead of life.

And Richmond loved them all.

Richmond could smell their need—smelled it behind the excrement, piss and body odor. He could smell it on stained breath as it passed broken teeth and bleeding gums. Richmond sensed his congregation long before he ever met them.

They were the same wherever he found them. People reduced to the basic instinct of need—he was simply a provider. He moved like a savior amongst the living damned. He healed them and took their pain.

He gave them visions.

And, of course, there was a price.

Jesus had charged a soul. One soul only—there was no bartering for miracles with the Jew child. Richmond asked his disciples for so much less: their loyalty.

Often was the occasion when he said to Scrye, "Even the broken need their pride. When they can wait for us it gives them purpose… and us power." Scrye was to take Richmond's place someday. And he would, for the money, not the esoteric of Richmond's belief.

"Why, Richmond? Out here in the middle of nothing. We don't even get money from the Freak. We don't…"

"We, Scrye, are the power for these privileged few. They worship us. You know that don't you? They worship our miracles. We are like Jesus amongst the lepers, gathering his disciples through the power of his workings. We are their angels."

Scrye opened his mouth to agree, but his mouth turned traitor.

"The Freak scares me Richmond. This whole thing seems wrong."

Richmond's cold glare swept like blue light from a pagan moon. "Fear is for the lesser man Scrye. Fear is for those weak in mind and purpose." A small smile—a glimpse of unhallowed insanity—broke open the flesh.

"Worry not. I always have..." With sudden ease a gun appeared in Richmond's hand. A sleight-of-hand trick that only a sociopathic magician would have taken the time to perfect. The cold silver gleamed in his palm with moonlit aura—King Arthur's holy sword Excalibur loaded with a clip.

Out of habit, Scrye's hand sought the comfort of his own steel. His gun was packaged far more mundanely, in a leather holster that unleashed its cargo far more simply, but just as effectively.

"Sorry, Richmond."

"It's alright Scrye. To forgive is to be Divine."

The gun disappeared, and silence filled the car. Scrye went back to watching the desert devour highway and sky in its slow creep across the world. Fingers of sand flexed out and touched the road. Everything was obliterated by a shifting maze of quartz and massive limestone plateaus that seemed to reach the horizon. Dark brown and windblown, the plateaus resembled the forgotten ruins that could have once been home to ancient, unnamed gods.

It was no surprise that Richmond was so at home here. The desert was the last of Earth's mysterious places. Richmond carried the Divine with him as surely as his gun. Was obsessed with it. Over the course of their travels, he had shown Scrye...things. Things with a capital 'T'—signs, sigils, omens—the supernatural

forced to obey reality. Scrye did his best to disbelieve, tried to ignore anything beyond the tangible. For Scrye, the world of saints
and angels, demons and devils, was reserved for those who had
never truly engaged in sin. The price of belief was salvation, or in
his case, damnation. The esoteric was dangerous in its implica-
tions. But Richmond made it hard, even impossible, to ignore his
words, especially in places like these. Hidden necropolises for the
forgotten wounded—lovers and junkies and suicides that didn't
have the courage or common sense to kill themselves. It was to
places like these that the fringes threw their unwanted. Places with
no names, people buried in the face of a common need, waiting to
be devoured.

He who walked amongst them was Richmond. Name spoken
like a rosary prayer; visage greeted like a vision.

Richmond brought the car to a halt as their destination revealed
itself. It was a small, ramshackle cluster of buildings half-buried in
the middle of a vast nothing. Tarpaulins and dirtied sheets acting
as walls flew and fluttered on a warm desert breath. The shelters
were huddled tightly together, like frightened children holding
hands for comfort. This made it difficult to tell where one dwelling
ended and another began. The buildings looked odd out here in
the middle of nothing—illusory and insubstantial. The landscape
that contained them a brown nightmare of sand that swelled like
slowly bloating flesh. The buildings themselves offered no sense
of comfort, hovering above that listless sea of sand, floating like
shadows.

Scrye opened the car door and stood beside Richmond. "What
are we doing? Why are we here? What in hell..."

"With their parlor tricks and talk of divinity, the prophets of old will pale in comparison. Out here we are the gods; we are those who provide the sacred for the profane."

As if on cue, a large, muscular man emerged from one of the dwellings, his body stained with black ink that formed strange totemic tattoos. Sinewy, healthy, a demigod of the addicted, the man called Freak saw to Richmond's affairs out in the desert. The Freak bowed deeply from the waist and spoke.

"Welcome, Richmond and little Scrye. Only not so little now. Time has laid his fleshless palms upon you and made you grow. Given you thoughts in your head." He bent down towards Scrye as though said thoughts might be visible and then abruptly turned. "We have been awaiting your arrival. The congregation will soon be present. The ritual will soon begin."

"Are they pure? Have they waited for me?" Richmond asked.

"Some have. Others have poisoned themselves with the cast-offs of the newcomers. Those who have transgressed have been separated. They await your judgment."

"Call them. Allow the ritual to begin. Call my flock that I may shepherd them and lead them from the darkness."

As the moon grew fat with pale light, the people began to leave their dwellings in long throngs of obedience shaped into straight lines. An area was sectioned off, made holy in the sand by the fact that Richmond had so deemed it, and was marked by long lines of flickering torches. Pock-marked arms screamed for puncture and fingers began a nervous twitching dance for spoon and needle. This was their ritual. The blood and bread distilled into cool liquid smack. The man, Richmond, brought them these miracles every few months, and they had shaped their needs in accordance.

Richmond walked amongst them, engaging in acts of parsimony with chemical miracles. Each member of the audience swayed in unison, small waves of devotion swelling like ocean water, rhythmic and divine, breaking upon the shore that was Richmond. He walked between those rows of flesh as Jesus had walked on water. Every eye strained to take him in and hold that vision in their hearts while their minds soared.

Their devotion was complete and whole. Their belief filled the air and soaked it with an angel-hair presence. Floating strands of gossamer impossibility rained from the sky, illuminated in the moonlight with white, flickering, snakelike movement. Heat was gathering, escaping from the baked sand beds into the cool desert night, and large plumes of mist filled the air.

Scrye was choked by the force of his disbelief trying to assert itself. He wanted to discount the supernatural birthing before his eyes, but could not find a way to do so. He had borne witness to the mundane miracles of flesh. He had seen men with speed-induced anger punch their soft fists through solid glass. Watched as boys filled with heroin, bodies shot to death and beyond, continued walking towards their aggressors with visionary eyes.

The fact that faith could become force did not surprise him.

The fact that faith was force did.

The gossamer rained down on Richmond, enveloping him with cocoon intentions. His body was enshrouded by the needs of the addicted faithful, and he was soon completely mummified. His flesh supped hungrily at it—absorbing it—flesh accepting spirit.

And then it was done. The congregation settled back, realizing that even a savior's work must come to an end. Richmond had come and pushed his everyday magic, and now the miracle was over.

Richmond shambled—a lurching, broken figure—from beyond

the reach of burning pools of light cast by the torches, and was quickly swallowed by darkness. Scrye staggered after him on shaky knees, the Divine making him weak and nauseous.

Richmond was now nowhere to be seen. Scrye walked deeper and deeper into the midnight desert. A cool wind pushed him forward and he did not fight it, shuffled blindly with its gentle insistence at his back. The sound of the desert, the hush of sand running over itself in invisible tides of graphite and quartz was all that broke the silence. There was no way Richmond could have come this far out. Scrye had seen him walking as though on feet broken by crucifixion.

An hour into the desert led Scrye to Richmond's body. He lay atop a small sand dune, his body twisted like a suicide jumper. Joints gleamed with white-exposed bone and blood-stained flesh. A sudden popping sound, like thick kindling snapping, and Richmond's body began an odd, epileptic dance. Liquid-filled sounds of opening flesh bubbled out in bright geysers of erupting blood. His skin split open in toothless smiles as odd growth tore the body apart. The air stank of puke, blood and shit—transformation revealing itself in odor. A hiss filled Scrye's ears, and his head screamed with the impossibility of the damnable sound.

"Sssss...sssss...ssScrye..." his name being hissed out, syllable by slow syllable, hanging in the air, waiting to be acknowledged. The body in front of him spread bloody lips and revealed rows of sharp, white teeth.

"It's real here, Scrye. It's real. The Word; their want—a world unto itself."

Fear rose from the pit of his stomach and stained Scrye's mouth with bile. "No." Negation was the only response he could allow himself. To say more would be to create the possibility that this nightmare world of belief could devour him.

"I am being. I am. I Am. I AM." A rising scream that brought the desert's winds to harsh life, whipping sand and dust. "I am belief made flesh. Want given wings." Richmond rose to his feet, gleaming with blood illuminated by moonlight. A sound of skin, wet music of growth, and two large shadows folded out from his back—black wings flexing in impossibility.

"I'm God, Scrye. God. Even Jesus couldn't fly."

Scrye stood shaking as the figure before him rose with monstrous wing strokes into an embracing sky.

"Can you believe now? Can I have your devotion? Belief is the price of salvation."

Angels and devils filled Scrye's response with horror. "I can't, Richmond. I cannot. Belief cannot touch me. Faith is not what I need." Biblical prophecy rained damnation in his ears, and he screamed to shut it out.

"Listen to me Scrye. Time is short. Soon the world will know my name. Already my presence taints their lips—cocaine lawyers and Valium housewives engaged in acts of unknowing prayer, calling me to their world. To be a God in the guise of a man. To be apocalypse before the old god could call for it."

Scrye's hand dropped south and drew his revolver with familiar intent. Six rapid flexes and flame and steel barked out death. Six cool squeezes, an empty gun, and a bloodless body. Black wings with shafts of moonlight bleeding through torn wings that healed quickly and cast pure, black shadows once again, like a promise of doom.

Scrye's hand went limp, and the gun fell to the sand. The desert began a rhythmic push, a *thump-thump* pulse, an organic movement.

"Can you feel that Scrye? It's my heart. MY FUCKING HEART."

Storm clouds bled into angry, red funnels that threw the desert sands into choking waves of dust. Scrye fell to his knees, searching blindly for his weapon. The steel was comfort if nothing else, a reminder of the sane world that was slowly slipping away. His fingers found the gun when Richmond's voice rang from on high.

"Take them both, Scrye. These are the articles of your faith. Discard them, they are useless." Richmond's gun fell with a low thud into the sand. Scrye picked it up, about to empty it into Richmond when the futility of the gesture made him scream. The violence it promised was useless.

Scrye turned and ran into the desert that was now beating like a madman's heart.

Thump-thump. Thump-thump.

When the blight of the dwellings on the horizon became visible, he slowed to a walk. Running would do him no good, he knew that. Time and distance could never save him from the horrors of...of Richmond's ascent from the real.

The entire populous was now visible, between 25 and 30 people on genuflected knee in a sectioned-off area whose boundaries were marked by three crucified people. The Freak sat at the head of the group, engaged in some arcane ritual. Scrye made his way to the car, a plan beginning to develop, a way to make the world ruled by flesh and blood again.

He had just finished feeding the gun and stuffing extra clips into his belt when the Freak's voice crept up from behind him.

"He said you would return, little Scrye, and so it has come to pass. Prophecy is the least of his powers now. Will you not come be humble amongst us?"

"Attendance isn't really a matter of choice anymore, is it?"

The Freak paused before responding. "There is always a choice, young Scrye. To believe, or to not believe. These are the only choices in any matter."

"Do you believe that he is a god, Freak? Do you really?"

"That no longer matters now. When Christ walked out from behind the shadow of that great stone with the stink of death on him, did it matter if he was truly divine? No, it did not. If Christ wasn't the Son of God when he was left for dead in that cave, he sure as hell was by the time he came out."

"Belief."

The Freak nodded slowly. "Come, Scrye. Let us join the congregation. Richmond will soon walk amongst us. Our place of honor awaits us at the front."

Scrye followed the Freak through a wall of sound, screams and odd prayer filling the air. Those above, the crucified, were singing songs orchestrated by their tortured nerves. Their pain expressed in a litany of broken flesh and screeching hot air forced from lungs seeking reprieve. Below that, in low keys of adoration, were the prayers of the faithful. Street slang mixed with the holy in an ode to the everlasting high.

Scrye's knees were beginning to pain when the Freak leaned over and whispered, "We are to become his angels, Scrye. Angels. This is our congregation and those crucified the sinners. We are to become myth along with Him."

The desert began to move again in an expanding fashion; sand began distending into huge waves that obliterated the horizon. As the sand approached, it broke open and surrounded them, forming vast walls of spinning, dizzying height.

From the center, directly in front of Scrye, the desert swelled. And up rose Richmond.

His head appeared first, shooting through the ground like a strange new tendril. The body followed after. Richmond stood, appraising his work as Scrye's eye was drawn to the new, hermaphroditic structure of Richmond's genitalia.

Black wings outspread, gleaming and beautiful, a prophet's dream of rapture. Richmond rose, slowly, levitating, pushing up on currents of air that swept downward, warmly caressing Scrye.

"Welcome to the new Eden my children. Welcome to the new Promised Land. You have called me, and I have answered. Witness the miracle."

The Freak crawled forward and spoke fervently, "These are the sinners placed before you, the few who did not believe in your return." He pointed to the crucified. "These are the few who tainted themselves with the cast-off of others. They await your judgment." A cowering gesture of fealty, and he returned to his spot beside Scrye.

"You have served me true and faithful, Freak. You will be amongst those who receive my blessing and hear the word directly. However, salvation and damnation must first be defined."

Those on the crosses began to wail louder as Richmond approached with strange pirouettes in the air. He pressed his hand against the forehead of a sobbing, naked, old man and spoke in a whisper that traveled like a scream.

"Do you believe?"

The man shrieked something wild. A prayer, a promise, an oath—Scrye couldn't tell.

Richmond placed his other hand against his own chest, fingers pinched together like a spider.

"Take and eat this, for this is flesh of my flesh." A circular segment of skin was torn out and placed into his gaping mouth. The man began to convulse as Richmond's hand left his forehead. An extreme and sudden arch in his spine tore the man from the cross with force, hands severed from the wrist in a gush of blood. The limbs rained red down onto the crowd as the body, suspended in air, began to twirl, feet over head, arms still extended in the aspect of crucifixion.

Richmond screamed from on high. "Damnation, Salvation and Judgment. Faith is what shall spare you. Faith is what will save you. My children, do you believe?"

A chorus of: "Yes."

"Now then, see the wages of sin."

As Scrye watched in horror, the body in the air began to discard its flesh. Flesh swirled off bone like skin from an apple forced by a knife. Twirling and peeling, large segments of tissue and protoplasm fell in a deluge. Musculature was all that was left—lustrous red meat that still wailed with torment. Sharp, white pieces of bone began to poke their way through bleeding crimson tissue as the body assumed a fetal position. Sharp, white points, thorns on flesh, broke out like some obscure desert star.

Richmond flew higher as Scrye pulled out his two guns. The sand in front of the second cross began a crawl towards its intended. The body was subsumed and then gone.

Richmond's voice thundered from the heavens. "Do you see, Scrye? I am the way. Believe in me. BELIEVE IN ME! Throw down your guns. Their power and your belief in them is NOTHING COMPARED TO ME!"

Scrye whispered, more to himself than for anyone to hear, "Salvation is for the sinless, Richmond." The muzzles of the guns softly kissed the side of the Freak's head and double chambers exploded. The top of his head disintegrated, and a small fragment of bone sliced open Scrye's cheek. Brain and viscera filled the air like a killer's dream of balloons.

Scrye stood and turned and began firing into the masses. A loop of gray intestine slicked through a bleeding layer of yellow fat as someone's stomach was ruptured by lead. Another man's teeth disappeared into the top of his head and blew out his cheeks in a puff of blood. Cartilage, bone, blood, puke and flesh showered Scrye's face as he worked through the crowd, pulling and pulling and pulling the triggers over and over and over again.

Above him, Richmond screamed. "God damn you, Scrye! I damn you!"

Bullet followed bullet, filling the air like a plague of locusts. People cowered at his feet as he shot them down.

A smile broke open on his face. To kill a god, one must find his cross. And so he had.

Richmond appeared directly above him, his face distressed and disappointed. "Death, Scrye. Only death for you." Richmond's right hand rose and pointed toward the sky. The desert sand assumed form and shot upward, an alkaline spike that punctured Scrye's right eye. He fell beside the spike, the jellied remains of his eyeball perched atop its point. A black hole disgorged blood from his head as blinded hands refilled the guns. Scrye stood again, and the people fell back in fear from him, this monster whom their God could not stop. Those who were left begged for Scrye's mercy.

Scrye pointed both of the guns at Richmond and emptied their chambers. Richmond fell screaming from the sky, the twirling star that had been the crucified man following after. The black wings that once carried him aloft folded in, dried out, and cracked open. They curled in on themselves, their thin membrane tearing open in jagged holes.

Scrye walked over and dropped to his knees in front of Richmond. The survivors crowded around them in a semi-circle of curiosity. Scrye placed a single bullet into each gun and placed both barrels in Richmond's mouth.

"I never wanted to believe, Richmond. You should not have asked that of me." And the guns decapitated the fallen angel. Scrye pursed his lips shut against the blood that erupted from the wounds, communion denied.

Those who had gathered around inched closer, wanting only to be near the spectacle. Scrye could feel the eyes of the last crucified man find him as the wall of sand that had surrounded the village fell into quiet dunes. The need to witness—an addiction far older than any drug—held them in its grasp.

Scrye pushed himself to his feet and began to walk. The villagers straggled behind him, wanting to remain close. The gaping hole in his head, filled with fiery pain and lost sight, was drowned out by a newer, more intense agony. Strange growths erupted through his back as large wings unfolded from metamorphosing flesh.

How ironic, he thought, that he who kills a god should become one in the process.

ABOUT THE AUTHOR
PAUL M. COLLRIN

Risking all the potential clichés that come with his daytime job, Paul Collrin is a proud high school English teacher by day and a dark fiction author after dusk arrives.

When not teaching the fine art of grammar to his students, Collrin can be found working on his current novel, recently completed during the summer of 2013.

Collrin's previous short story publications include "Dreams of Flesh and Bone," which can be found in *Cthulhu Sex Magazine*, and "Broken" which was published in the Chimericana anthology titled *All Cars Must Die*.

PARTY GUESTS
CHAD STROUP

1. Now Not Then

Call me Geoffrey. Why? Well, 'cause that's the name Pops gave me. Also called me 'Idiot Genius.' Don't like that name. Sometimes I have bad, bad dreams. Red dreams. Real dreams.

Got four people collected in my house today—well it's more of an apartment, well it's more of a four-hundred-square-foot studio. Program helped me get a job over at the Dollar Tree so I can pay rent, buy Flamin' Hot Cheetos, lick the orange-red fire spice off my fingers. Watch dirty movies on my cable TV I paid for myself. Momma can't tell me not to now. Been gone a long time.

Sally's my neighbor, real pretty with hair color like pineapple-upside-down cake. Rosie worked at my group home, then she was my job coach, now she's at my house. She's kinda chocolate in the face like Oprah, but she don't make so much money. Brought me my old video games. *Grand Theft Auto. Dance Dance Revolution.*

Met Kim and Daryl out in the community at the Taco Bell by the bus stop on 10th Avenue. Kim's got a nice double bubble. Don't usually invite boys, but Daryl had to come 'cause he's her son. Hope he likes game shows. All that's on right now. *Family Feud. Super Password. Press Your Luck.* Big bucks, no whammy. No *Kojak* cop shows. No *Mi Vida Loca* gang shows. Not supposed to watch those. Too many red thoughts. No *Legend of the Overfiend* anime tentacle shows. Too many scream dreams. Too many surprise sex dreams. Too many dig-dry scab dreams.

One. Two. Three. Four. Piled on my floor. Need to get the table set. Shiny silverware. No spots. No dirt. No filth. Wash hands. Scrub hands. Bleed raw hands. Corpse friends.

Doctor says I'm autistic, but I ain't never drawn no pictures.

Like to spray sweet cinnamon scent when it gets real stale in here. Got a case of twenty-four cans. Lasts me a month or so. Twenty dollars, real good deal. Don't like urine smell much. Don't like rot smell any better.

One thousand five hundred twenty-three jellybeans in the jar. No eating black. Like the green ones.

Done some awful things in my life. "Today's the Devil's Playground," like Rosie used to say. Rosie's non-verbal now. Gotta get some treats ready. Like to serve appetizers. Nipple hors d'oeuvres. Tongue filet mignon. Intestine pasta with cream skin sauce. Blender was a good Christmas gift last year. Thanks Gramma.

Quick snack of eyes like seedless grapes. Not Daryl though. Still want him to watch TV with me. Like Kim's silky hair. Want to scalp her like an Injun would. Want to make her my girlfriend. Had a girlfriend once. Had sex once. Name was Yolanda, but she met another boy named Travis last year. Not supposed to talk about past events though.

Geoffreybadverybad. Had another scary dream last night, is this it? Not sure I can control it or if I care either way. Time-Out Room no fun.

Preacher says my moral compass faces south.

Stupid cable's going out again. Don't like snow. Real stuff's not supposed to be here. Why's it on my TV now making scratchy itchy noise? Need to change channel. Watch Rambo gun shows. Like Chuck Norris kill shows. Can't find remote control. Square root of 13 is 3.605551275463.

2. BusStopGo

Diesel fuel's in the same risk group as asbestos and arsenic. Bus number 15 stops two blocks from my old group home. Number 15 stops every 15 minutes. Turned 15 years old in the group home. 2925 Zephyr Road. 2+9+2+5= 18. Was 18 when Pops died. Didn't care much. Pops was a cock-knuckle. Mad cow. Necrotizing fasciitis. Drowned in the kiddie pool after too much vodka. Elephantiasis of the bunghole. Asbestos, arsenic, diesel fuel. Who knows? Not me.

Don't live at 2925 Zephyr no more. 744 Navajo now. Twenty-one years old now. Independent now. Big chief of my teepee. Tickle-feather teepee. Scratchy-leather teepee. Don't want to see Mary or Jacobus or Mondo or Alice or Keiko or Terry or no one else from my group home. Maybe Rosie though. Always liked Rosie. Treated me like a person.

I remember once Rosie says, GEOFFREY YOU'RE SUCH A BIG, HARMLESS, SQUISHY TEDDY BEAR. IT'S HARD NOT TO LIKE YOU. WHEN YOU'RE BEHAVING APPROPRIATELY, THAT IS. Also used to say I was a client, a consumer. Only to other people at the group home and the transition program though. Average 'merican consumes 85.5 pounds of fat and oil every year, 141.6 pounds of caloric sweeteners. Got that beat by a big, big lot. Shows how much Rosie knows. Not just a person, I'm motherfucking Superman.

Right?

Right.

Jacobus always called Rosie *N* word. Not supposed to use *N* word. Jacobus got put in Time-Out Room for saying *N* word three times. Don't like Time-Out Room. Cold, white pillow walls. Try to avoid Time-Out Room. Dingy, spotty window. Can't open, can't break. Tempered glass. Why you so mad, glass? Maybe 'cause last Tuesday, Nando Gutierrez smeared hot, brown shit on the Time-Out Room window. Don't want to think about what's prob'ly in the crackies of the pillow walls. Ain't mine.

On the bus now. Passing by the Bank of 'merica. Where I take my paychecks. Mucky, creamy stucco walls. Number 15 stops across from AM/PM at Fifty-fifth and Maple. Gonna get a chili dog. Two chili dogs with onion, one with no chili. Maybe some nachos. Extra jalapeños please. Tongue on fire. Spicy icy. Thank you, come again.

Bus stop again now. In front of AM/PM. Gotta go back the way

I came. Save one chili dog in my pocket for later. Homeless man creepin' on the side of AM/PM with his pit bull doggie. Ain't gettin' my snacks. Fuck that noise.

Transfer to Number 10. Take me to Dollar Tree. Dollar Tree on 10th Avenue. Number 10 stops on 10th. Start work at 10 A.M. Maybe get ten tacos at Taco Bell for ten dollars. Five for first break, five for second break. Five minute breaks. Steal five packs of Little Debbie Swiss Rolls. No stealing tapes. No stealing tapes.

Got my Sony Walkman. Listen to my Willie D *Controversy* tape. Like the song "Bald Headed Hoes." Good music. Good words. Yeah.

> *"Something must be done about these citizens.*
> *You ask what will I do to support my fellow man?*
> *I'm proposing a bill to Capitol Hill*
> *to kill all bald headed women at will."*

You tell 'em, Will. I'm a damn good rapper just like you.

On bus Number 10 now. Young girl sitting across from me. Not bald. Hair like a firecracker explosion and red, red, red like Ronald McDonald. Chicken nuggets with honey dip. Yum. Girl's face real friendly. No, real scary to Geoffrey. Eyes. Black, black circle eyes. Target eyes. Dagger rings in ears. Want to pull them. Stab them. Purple-People-Eater lips. Want to pinch them. Itch them. Funny look says she don't like my rapping though. So what? Want to know what her mushy mounds taste like. Want to know what her bad parts look like.

NO!

Rock back and forth, Geoffrey. Do the pigeon dance, Geoffrey. Just listen to the Willie D tape, Geoffrey. Don't look at scary, cutie young girl, Geoffrey. Probably got three boyfriends anyways. Maybe use another one? Don't mind. Free for all kinds of naked, pumpy time. Hand gets tired. Rub, rub raw.

Young girl's shirt torn and light black and says, "CHARGED G.B.H." Look it up later on public library computer. Thirty-minute limit. Leave ID at front desk. No Hentai. No penetration. No nudes. L.O.L. Look up CHARGED G.B.H. Computer's got pictures of peacock pogo hair men. Music sample. Noise sample. Singing/screaming. Axing/playing. Beating/pounding. Computer says, "Grievous Bodily Harm." Like the idea. Scribble it, put it in my pocket. Probably good didn't mess with bus girl. Cotton-candy-prison witchy or somethin'.

Not Geoffrey's type. Someone better out there to love. Someone better to keep in my pocket.

3. Chalupa After Work

No damn tacos for Geoffrey today.

Motherfucker Fat Register Bee-yotch says, WE'RE OUT OF SOUR CREAM.

Asked for soft taco with no meat, add beans, no lettuce, extra cheese. Fat Fucko don't like that order, yells at me. Don't care. Just keep rapping. Waiting for Chalupa, waiting for Cinnamon Twists. Drinking Mountain Dew Code Red. Refills. Threefills.

Feather hair sexy lady comes in. Motorboat. Cunnilingus. Make whoopee on *The Newlywed Game*. Little boy comes in too. Who cares? I ain't no Michael Jackson.

"The kid is not my son."

You tell 'em, Mikey. Don't want no stinkin' baby neither.

Lady and boy see Fatty being all mad, yelling at me. For taking too much fire sauce. Out of mild sauce. What do they expect?

Lady says, SO WHAT? LEAVE HIM ALONE! Then she whispers and says, "can't you see he's special?"

No high-frequency loss on the audiogram test. Got ears like a barn owl. Hoot! Hoot!

Then Lady says to me, ARE YOU OKAY? YOU POOR THING. WHAT KIND OF AN AWFUL PERSON WOULD YELL AT A BIG SWEETHEART LIKE YOU? I OUGHT TO COMPLAIN TO HER MANAGER. She says that last part in a dragon voice while lookin' all mean over at Fatty.

Thought she was gonna pull an Auntie Betty and pinch my fat ass cheeks. Guess that'd be okay. As long as she don't jiggle my jellyrolls. Hate that. Scratch that.

I say, YEAH. I'M COOL. I'M GEOFFREY. YOU'RE PRETTY. PRETTY *NICE*.

Lady laughs. Maybe 'cause Geoffrey's smooth, maybe 'cause she gets the joke. Turns all blushy, then says, THANKS, GEOFFREY. I'M KIM AND THIS IS MY SON DARYL. CAN YOU SAY HI, DARYL?

Daryl hides under the booth and says, HI, DARYL, then plays with dumb robot toy and says, DANGER WILL ROBINSON!

I say, WHY'S HE WEARING A SUIT? IS TODAY CHURCH DAY?

Kim sighs and says, WELL, GEOFFREY—DARYL'S SPECIAL. SORT OF LIKE YOU. HE HAS TOURETTE'S SYNDROME. DO YOU KNOW WHAT THAT IS?

I nod. I shrug. She don't notice. Just keeps yapping.

She says, IT'S NOTHING TO BE ASHAMED OF. HE JUST

DOESN'T LIKE TO WEAR ANYTHING BUT BLUE SUITS. RE-
FUSES, TO BE HONEST.

I say, OK, FAIR ENOUGH.

Daryl says, BUTTERMILK! FUCKERMILK! maybe three times
before momma shushes him.

She says, AND HE CURSES. A LOT. DO YOU NEED ANY
HELP, GEOFFREY? A RIDE SOMEWHERE?

I say, MAYBE.

Eating my Chalupa. Finally. Damn. Kim and me talk about poli-
tics. The government. Budget Christmas. *HA!* No we don't. Stupid. Don't watch the news. Too busy for the news. Gotta catch up
on watching my *Street Sharks* tape. Stole it from Amvets. News
boring. Don't care about president. Geoffrey's got a life. Watch
Charles Bronson *Death Wish 3* instead.

Wanna feel Kim's soft, soft, silky follicles in my fingers. Wanna
tear real quick like a Band-Aid. Wanna see the itty-bitty red drops
on the bald, bald scalp. Take 15 hairs, mix and match the shades.
Find the longest one. Put it in my pocket, save for later on Bus 15.

Invite Kim and Daryl to my house—well it's more of an apartment, well it's more of a four-hundred-square-foot studio. Can't
come. *Damn!*

Daryl got homework, therapy, something. *Damn.* Give me a
ride to my house anyways. Not far. Better than Bus 15. Stop by
the AM/PM first. Get some Pop Rocks. Put the Pop Rocks in my
Mountain Dew Code Red. *Boom!*

Drop me off. Take my phone number. Gonna answer their call
on my Marvin the Martian phone.

*"Oh, I can hardly wait till Hugo finds him. Hugo will be so
thrilled, he will probably smother him with love."*

You tell 'em, Marv. That Daffy Duck is a damn pussy.

Say they'll come by this weekend. Bring me lunch. I say, OK.

Wonder if it'll be an Ultimate Cheeseburger. Or a meatball sammich and Funyuns. Or a breakfast burrito. For lunch.

4. Did You Know?

Monday's the most popular day to kill yourself in the Netherlands. Today's Tuesday. Where the hell are the Netherlands? Is that near Disneyland? Fuck Mickey. No. Wait. Fuck Minnie. Little slut mouse. *Ha.*

'Proximately 178 seeds on a McDonald's Big Mac bun. 1+7+8=16. Was 16 when I had my first Shamrock Shake. Green-ass tongue. Grimace is my homeboy.

Cockroach heads can live for days—no, weeks—without fucking bodies. Prob'ly true. Kicked one once. Hard. Body stayed there. Head and two front legs kept on truckin'. Sucka had somewhere important to be.

Almonds are members of the peach family. Aw, nuts.

Ear, eye, gum, jaw, hip, arm, leg, toe, rib, lip. All human body parts. Three letters long. Three guests in my house right now. Daryl don't count.

Ketchup leaves the bottle at 25 miles per year. Red, red flow slow. Be 46 years old when ketchup's done spilling. 4 times 6 is 24. Three pretty ladies in my house. 24 minus 3 is 21. 21 years old now.

Thirty minutes up?

Screw you, library lady.

Be back next week anyways.

5. *Won't You be My Neighbor?*

Little Miss Sally likes to sunbathe on the patio. Undoes her bikini top so sun can fill in white, white holes, make her back all dark like J. Lo. Sally from the block. Sally on the chopping block.

Thanksgiving turkey. Take your pick. Dark meat, please. *"Different flavor means different savor,"* like Gramma used to say. Mashed mashy taters with butter and gravy. Squirt, squirt, squirt in the sausage stuffing. Soft, squishy crescent rolls like baby legs. No green bean casserole. Tastes like hot, summer ass-crack.

Sometimes get out my X-Ray Specs, peek through the blinds. Sally's already naked. What's the point? Make-Believe Land. Funfunfun.

Gristle missile, blood flood, bone moan.

Give myself the Bad Touch. Gramma would slap my behind red, red, red if she knew about the Bad Touch. Gramma died last month. Can't say much now. Tombstone talk.

Sally's hair hangs off the side of her chair. Can't count from here. Blondes average about 140,000 strands on their heads. Means 383.561643836 hairs every day this year. Works for me. Keep me busy. *"Idle hands do Devil's work,"* like Rosie used to say. Can't help myself with the Bad Touch. Makes me miss Yolanda. Not really, though. Played Dr. Salami with Yolanda once. Just once. Real good time.

Told Yolanda, I DON'T WANT NO BABY CHILD.

Then gave her a little slap in the eye.

Yolanda's non-verbal. Don't know her opinion. Who cares? She can tell it to her PECS book.

Guess everything worked out. No damn baby. No damn squirty,

crying, stinky shit trashcan brat. Yolanda got her menstruation. Likes to eat her menstruation blood. Fresh or dry. Don't matter much. Bad, bad behavior. Not appropriate. Has to wear Ripstop Jumpsuit for a few days. Maybe stupid Travis will 'pregnate her later. Good luck, Travis. Gonna need it.

Can't make baby with Bad Touch Special Time. *Phew!*

Maybe Sally wants baby. Maybe not. Worth risk of nookies and cookies. Want to rub her double bubble. Wash hands clean. Brush teeth. Floss teeth. Dig in fingernails with scrub brush. No fingerprints on soft, soft skin. Lick, lick leather. Rub, rub raw. Shave with grain. Against grain. Grain matter, grey matter, brain matter. Teeny, tiny toilet-paper spots sop blood drops. Leave mustache to look like *Magnum, P.I.*

Sally goes and gets dressed. Go knock on her door five minutes later. Gotta let the woman have her time. Takes forever. Two forevers. Gotta look presentable for Geoffrey. Look across the street while waiting. What's goin' on? Man mowing lawn. Sweaty ass. Severed grass. Green, green blade make clean flesh flayed.

Sally opens door. Looks like a cupcake angel. Has a tank top that says "LOVE PINK" on it. Shirt has purple/white stripes, though. Don't get it.

Sally says, OH. HI GEOFFREY. HOW ARE YOU DOING TODAY?

I say, SALLY, WHAT YOU THINK ABOUT BABIES?

She says, ARE YOU KIDDING? O. M. G. I'M TOO YOUNG TO THINK ABOUT THAT, GEOFFREY. I'LL WAIT UNTIL I'M MARRIED. I DON'T EVEN HAVE A STEADY BOYFRIEND RIGHT NOW.

I say, DAMN SHAME SALLY. STUPID MEN. THEY BLIND.

YOU DON'T HAVE A HUSBAND IN FIVE YEARS GIVE ME A CALL. DON'T LIKE BABIES MUCH, THOUGH. JUST SAYIN'.

Sally laughs and says, OKAY, GEOFFREY. THAT'S, UH, SWEET OF YOU TO SAY. I'LL KEEP THAT IN MIND.

I say, YOU GOT MY NUMBER, RIGHT?

Sally nods. Then I say, CAN YOU COME OVER LATER, HELP ME WITH MY CHECKBOOK? GOT MY PAYCHECK TODAY. GOTTA PAY CABLE. BILLS MAKE ME CUCKOO FOR COCOA PUFFS.

She says, I THINK SO. I CAN TRY TO COME BY AFTER I GO TO THE GYM, IF THAT'S COOL.

Don't know who Gym is. Don't like him very much already.

6. *Goodboy*

One time, when I was ten or eleven or twelve, Pops gave my behind a real good swat. Found me playing with some neighbor's roadkill cat on side of the road. Cadaver. Cataver. Shitty kitty. Poked it with a dead, dead stick. Eyeball all gravy gooey. Peel back the furry layers like Velcro. Pops beat me real good. Never messed with no dead cats again. Too much trouble. Plenty of other dead things to play with anyways. Pops would be proud. *No he wouldn't.* Don't care though. Pops was a dicksicle. Sent me off to group home—2925 Zephyr. Made me go to special school. Goldberg Education Center—67 67th Street. Coincidence? Hell no.

Teacher says to Pops, WELL, ACCORDING TO DR. SORIAN, YOUR SON IS VERY GIFTED IN MANY WAYS. FOR INSTANCE, AS YOU PROBABLY ALREADY KNOW, HE HAS THE ABILITY TO PERFORM A VARIETY OF COMPLICATED MATHEMATICAL

EQUATIONS IN HIS HEAD. Then she whispers and says, "he also has severe autism and has been diagnosed as being e.d."

But I hear that shit. I say, NO WAY. I *HATE* REESE'S PIECES.

Teacher looks all shocked at my superpowers and says, GEOFFREY, I'M NOT SURE WHAT YOU THINK YOU HEARD, BUT I'M MERELY TELLING YOUR FATHER THAT YOU'VE BEEN DIAGNOSED AS EMOTIONALLY DISTURBED. IT'S OKAY. IT'S NOTHING TO BE ASHAMED OF. Then she turns back to Pops and says, WE'LL PLACE HIM IN THE REGULAR ELEMENTARY CLASSROOMS FOR NOW. WHEN HE TURNS EIGHTEEN HE CAN ENTER THE TRANSITION PROGRAM, AND THEN HE'LL GRADUATE WHEN HE TURNS TWENTY-ONE. WE'VE GOT SOME GREAT PROGRAMS TO HELP SOMEONE SPECIAL LIKE YOUR SON LEARN HOW TO FUNCTION AND ASSIMILATE INTO SOCIETY.

7. Come on Barbie Let's Go Party

Rosie says I shouldn't look at porno. Plastic women. Placid flaccid. Caught me once on computer when we were at my group home. Not my apartment. 2925 Zephyr. Not 744 Navajo.

Penetration shot. Porno clown lick, lick, licking all over naked nipples like a wannabe Gollum. Money shot. Monkeyshine. Midget ass.

I say, CAN YOU FIT A WATERMELON IN ONE OF THOSE?

Rosie says, NO GEOFFREY. THAT'S NOT APPROPRIATE.

Once, when Rosie was my job coach, we were at Dollar Tree. Working. Dusting shelves. Dust is made of dead skin cells, dried feces, desiccated corpses of dust mites, and tiny fibers of clothing.

Stealing dusty 3 Musketeers. Love, love nougat.

I say, ROSIE, DO THEY HAVE NUDIE MAGS HERE?

She says, NO GEOFFREY. THAT'S NOT APPROPRIATE.

Rosie didn't talk much, talks even less at my party. Kinda liked her. Never called her *N* word.

One time I said, ROSIE, THERE'S A PARTY IN MY PANTS. YOU'RE INVITED.

Rosie didn't get the joke, didn't work with me much for a little while. Tried to transfer to the adult program site. Threatened to take away my games. *Mortal Kombat. Paperboy.* Had to apologize. Later. Much later alligator.

Still good friends, me and Rosie. Like a decoration friend, not a roommate friend.

8. *Gay Nando Commando*

Nando Gutierrez tried to kiss me. No way, buddy. Don't play that sloppy-ass, man-tongue game. Never even let Yolanda kiss me. Hate lips. Hate spit.

I say, NANDO, CUT IT OUT.

Nando says, I'D LIKE MORE MILK, PLEASE.

Nando Gutierrez scream, scream squawks like a macaw. Don't like that much. Not the best guy to talk to. Don't take 'no' for an answer. Oh well...

Nando Gutierrez eats Cap'n Crunch with no milk instead of doing his schoolwork. Task avoidance.

I say, NANDO, WHERE'S YOUR MILK?

Nando says, MORE EGGS, PLEASE.

I say, NANDO, I GOT A SIX PACK OF SURGE IN MY ROOM. TRADE YOU FOR YOUR DISCMAN.

Nando says, SURE, GEFFY.

Nando Gutierrez don't like to haggle much. Like that about him. Ain't invited to my party, though. Don't want boys there. Farmer John's Sausage Fest. Nando can stay at home and watch *The Electric Company* for all I care.

Nando Gutierrez run, run, runs like a wing-flapping fool. Jacobus or Keiko laughed about something else, made Nando have a behavior. Nando's about as giant as a black rhinoceros. Good luck getting Nando in prone position. Rhino horns are made of keratin, a fibrous protein that forms the structure of hair. Harder to count than pretty lady hair though. Or easier? Don't know.

Glad I'm high functioning. Glad I'm independent. Lucky duck.

I say, NANDO, YOU AIN'T A BIRD.

Nando stops. Seems kinda normal. Just for a second.

9. Little Buddy

Daryl's on my big comfy recliner. Suit could use a wash. Lookin' a little lousy. Lookin' like a tiny business elf that just got fired and sauced and picked a scrap with a fake, orange-fingernailed toothless ho.

He says, WHERE'S MY MOM AT?

I say, SHE'LL BE RIGHT BACK. JUST WENT TO VONS TO GET GRAPE JUICE OR SOMETHING.

Daryl says, BUTTERMILK PANCAKES! LICK A DICK! GEOFFREY, MY HANDS HURT.

I say, DON'T WORRY ABOUT IT DARYL. WANNA WATCH *DOUBLE DARE*? IT'S A MARATHON.

Super, sloppy, oozy slime. Creamy grime. Ice-cream time.

10. †††

Had another scary dream last night, is this still it? Shitshitshit. Spray my cinnamon cans all over the apartment. Last can. Empty can. Need to buy more. Better still be on sale. Smells real bad. Like someone dumped in here, then ate it, then puked it all up, then spooged on top of it. Copper smell. Salty bleach smell. Wonder why? Had a dream last night. Broke into a foxy, fucky girl's house. Surprise sex dream.

Red dream.

Kill dream.

Skin dream.

Don't know if I could control myself if it was a real dream.

ABOUT THE AUTHOR
CHAD STROUP

Chad Stroup is currently pursuing his MFA in Fiction at San Diego State University.

His work has recently been featured in the *San Diego Poetry Annual, Educe Journal, Penduline* and the anthology *Enter at Your Own Risk: Fires and Phantoms*.

Stroup is the editor and co-author of the collaborative text, "Art Making in the Technosphere," that was featured in *Fiction International #46* and was nominated for the Pushcart Prize and the AWP Intro Journals Award.

His blog, *Subvertbia*, is a showcase of some of his peculiar short fiction and poetry.

THE VISCERA OF WORSHIP
ALLEN GRIFFIN

When I left my home for the unknown highways, I didn't know there were others like me in the world. My parents worshipped a more conventional god, yet their strict discipline often strayed into corporal punishment. The blood they drew from me spoke with its own voice. It spoke with the voice of Leviathan. Leaving behind a life of opulence, I sought out the animal realities our civilization attempted to mask—the snakes swimming through the subconscious depths of humanity.

Yet there I was, staring across a dying campfire at the weather-worn face of a man named Barbas, who claimed an intimate, masterful knowledge of our bloodthirsty, dark god Leviathan. I cursed my status as an aspirant, but bathed in the glow of the company offered by my newfound companion.

Barbas discovered me as I was worshipping in the woods, a
drifter's entrails spread throughout the clearing, arranged in a
crude, yet sacred, geometry of my mysticism. I didn't possess the
skill of an adept, the ability to eat the flesh and consume the souls
of victims as required by Leviathan, but my intent was unquestionable. This was an act of veneration, an attempt to be noticed by
the god I worshipped. As Barbas watched, I could see the serenity
on his face, and I instantly knew I could trust him.

When the ritual was complete, we set off together, walking for
miles through the forest. Birds and insects fell silent as we passed.
At one point Barbas stopped and spoke to me.

"Nothing creates life like death, and nothing tastes as glorious
as torn flesh between your teeth."

We then pressed on without uttering another word for hours,
eventually crossing the highway and reentering the woods. We
hiked deep into the forest until we were far from the logging roads.
Finally, we set up camp and built another small fire.

Beneath the stars, the true face of Barbas began to reveal itself,
his features amorphous in the light of the moon. The play of shadow and light revealed his reptilian eyes, and rats climbed through
the pores of his skin. It was obvious that I was in the presence of
a great master. I could hear movement in the foliage all around—
predators and carrion feeders stared at us from the darkness. I
couldn't tell if the beasts were fearful or reverent.

"I will show you how to find what you seek," Barbas said.

He dug in the pockets of his dilapidated coat until he produced
a severed finger adorned with a ring of intricate, writhing, plati-
num circles. My eyes ached as I gazed upon it. He pulled the ring
off the finger, placed it between his lips and swallowed it. He then

stuck the digit in his mouth and chewed. I could hear the crack of brittle bones between his teeth. His eyes were closed, and he seemed to savor the taste.

Barbas opened his eyes and, for a pregnant moment, stared up at the stars. Breaking his upward gaze, he leaned over and began to retch violently onto the ground. A pool of vomit, blood and offal spread across the dirt, and he motioned for me to gaze into the liquid.

I immediately became lost in the visions bestowed to us by Leviathan. A portion of the sky rained down upon me like a waterfall, coating my skin in a viscous liquid. Wiping the sludge from my eyes, I saw a landscape of blood and flesh, a holy land, a destination for my visionary pilgrimage. Invisible bodies writhed against my skin. I found the sensation pleasurable, like the cold lips of dead lovers kissing me.

I was consumed in a rapture of exquisite suffering as I beheld towers of flesh shooting geysers of blood into the night sky. A swath of stars appeared, stained crimson and illuminating a path towards the horizon. In slow motion, Barbas pointed into the distance, indicating to me the way forward.

I followed the direction of his finger and saw not only a physical journey but a spiritual one as well, the path to my initiation. I gathered my things and headed east, back towards the highway.

* * *

Several hours passed before I was able to hitch a ride. Perhaps I had failed to disguise the aura of death that clung to me even tighter than my filthy clothes.

As the sun began to set, and I contemplated another night sleeping under the stars, a black eighteen-wheeler pulled to the side of the road. An arm emerged from the window, the driver motioning for me to climb aboard.

Piloting the behemoth was a diminutive, old man who introduced himself as Floyd. He looked to be a century old and couldn't have weighed much more than a hundred pounds. I wondered if he truly possessed the strength to turn the steering wheel of the massive truck.

My concerns quickly became irrelevant as he maneuvered the big rig back onto the highway. We drove with gathering speed toward the darkening horizon. Floyd chain-smoked and chattered incessantly.

"I don't pick up just anyone," Floyd stated at one point, "But you looked like a snake caught in the headlights. Usually the only person who rode with me was my wife, but she is resting in her God's cold, wet embrace now."

"We should one day all be so lucky," I replied.

As the hours passed I found myself staring at Floyd, his eyes never leaving the road ahead. The reflection of passing headlights bounced off a large, gold chain that hung around his neck and disappeared beneath his collar. While something about the jewelry beckoned me, I was repulsed by the man himself. His slight frame was sickening, and I quickly grew weary of his babble.

"There is no warmth compared to my mother's entrails," I blurted out impatiently, "my soul was stillborn and my placenta was a garbage bag."

"Son, I reckon you're one helluva poet," Floyd said.

At first, I feared my irritability would cost me my ride. Instead, we drove on, the cab of the truck having slipped into silence. Floyd seemed to have no intention of kicking me out. I found myself staring at the crimson path in the sky above, and ahead I could see the glow of city lights on the horizon.

On the outskirts of the city, Floyd pulled the big rig over into the emergency lane.

"The city lights are shining brighter than the stars, son." He nodded towards the passenger door, indicating I should get out. I didn't protest, and frankly I was glad he had taken me as far as he had after my outburst. Although, it did occur to me that he should be thankful I hadn't painted my flesh with his blood.

Before I shut the door, Floyd spoke again. "I'll be at Chilly's Truck Stop on the south side of town in three days. You need a ride out of this gutter or anything, come see me."

* * *

Two uneventful days passed and I grew despondent. Barbas had given me the gift of revelation, and I followed the stars to what I assumed would be my initiation, but the trail had now gone cold. I slept beneath an overpass and spent my time begging for food. My guiding stars were obscured by the veil of light pollution. I saw no omens to guide me any further.

I lusted for blood sacrifice, wishing to find some way to regain the favor of Leviathan. Manna, however, proved hard to come by. People in this place were wary of predators, or were predators themselves.

I subsisted on a diet of animal flesh cooked over burning piles of garbage. This mostly consisted of rats, or the occasional pet snatched from a yard. The meat tasted like newspaper and burnt plastic.

It wasn't until the third day that my pilgrimage began to regain some of its lost momentum. Walking the streets, I caught the scent of the viscera of worship wafting through the night air. I followed the aroma into an alley.

A black van sat idling with its lights off. On the pavement next to the vehicle, a tangle of bodies writhed in the gore of a mutilated corpse, feeding in the ways of the initiated. When I approached they froze, and their glowing eyes cast lecherous gazes at me.

I sensed an aesthetic beauty to the kill, a symmetry I could barely grasp. The victim's body was twisted into a sigil, releasing both its flesh and soul into a state upon which they could be consumed. Looking back on my own murders, I felt a sense of embarrassment at their crudeness.

I knew these were my people, and yet they fled, leaping into the van and flipping on its headlights. I ran to the side door before it slid shut, and I was greeted by the blood-stained face of a young woman.

"Unworthy!" she screeched.

She lifted her crimson-stained t-shirt above her midriff, revealing a tapestry of scars that twisted upon itself like a ball of snakes. She had no belly-button.

"Life lover!" She condemned me. I could think of no greater denouncement. I spat on the meager gift of life, to be unaware of the dark depths within us, depths left unexplored with the dim light of consciousness.

My judgment passed, the van drove off and shot down the alley, ejecting itself into the intersection beyond.

I was left again to the streets, even lonelier than before. I imagined I saw the van at distant intersections, heard the cry of the young woman with the belly full of reptiles. The entire city seemed to reek of the violence and death I yearned for, but I was turned away. I wished only to be worthy, to know the ritual methods of the initiated.

The city seemed to revel in murder, but excluded me from its rites. Smog draped over the buildings. I imagined the streets heaving in a sacrificial ritual climax. It was all too much. I couldn't stay if my own kindred souls wouldn't count me among their number.

The open road would be my seminary. I would spill blood until my worthiness was unquestionable, until I saw the patterns and fed upon the souls of my victims. The time came to leave.

I made my way back to Chilly's and back to Floyd to take him up on his offer of a ride out of the city. My head hung low as the traffic passed. I felt alone, trapped between the pathetic masses and the exalted initiates. I swore I wasn't giving up, but merely regrouping. My will was weak and I was unsure of what my truth was in that moment.

Floyd's tractor-trailer sat in the shadow-drenched corner of the truck stop. Above, the moon danced in and out of the clouds, bathing the landscape in a slow strobe that seemed to point me towards the rig. Periodically, Floyd's cigarette glowed brighter as he took a drag from inside the cabin.

The passenger door was unlocked as if he anticipated my arrival. I climbed into the cab without invitation.

"I thought I might see you again," he said, chuckling to himself as he smashed the cigarette out in the ashtray. He flashed an idiotic smile, baring yellow-stained teeth.

I waited for the engine to turn over, but Floyd just stared out the window, absently lighting another cigarette.

"City's a rough place if you don't know the right people." He paused to take a drag. His shirt was unbuttoned and he scratched his belly. "You remember me talking about my wife? She would've simply loved you. Birds of a feather..." Trailing off. "Birds of a god-damn feather."

He turned to face me, his gold chain catching the available light. The pendant on the end lay on his sunken sternum. The gold was cast in the same shape as the ball of serpents I saw etched in scars on the woman's abdomen. Gazing upon the object, I saw within it the secrets of Leviathan's mysticism.

"Some worship the Dark God," Floyd said, "others of us are just manna for his initiates."

I slid my knife from my jacket and into my hand, and just as smoothly, slid the blade into Floyd's belly. He didn't scream. Instead, his eyes slowly rolled back into his head, and a slight smile crept across his face. I sat silently, savoring the feeling of warm blood washing over my hand. I watched Floyd as his life slipped away.

Afterwards, I broke his bones and feasted on his organs, twisting him into the fractal nightmares revealed by the pendant. I now understood the secret, and his soul—his sacrifice—revealed the path to me once more.

* * *

Stalking the city with renewed vigor, I wrote my contribution to the dark grimoire of the night on the pavement like blood-scrawled graffiti. My own predatory eyes guided me through the streets as I now became the hunter I had always longed to be.

I left a trail of sacrifice in my wake. Some were like frightened animals, while others who had thought they lived at the top of the food chain learned their rightful place at the end of my blade. Ultimately, they all became my manna.

I knew eventually the pack wouldn't be able to resist the scent of chum in the water. And soon the black van began to appear and disappear. It circled me warily, like a beast investigating its prey.

With my confidence restored and Floyd's pendant burning with blood passion, I gathered the sacrificial bodies in a derelict row house on a vacant block where even the rats had fled my presence. Inside the building I sat in a meditative posture among the broken geometry of corpses. Severed limbs were carefully placed on the floor, broken bones speared into limbless torsos, the victims twisted and reshaped into sigils of worship.

Outside, under the setting sun, the van rumbled at the curb, the sound of its exhaust seeping into the periphery of my consciousness. But inside was eternal midnight. All around me was a blackened void that thrived, taking on a life of its own behind boarded-up windows. Controlling my emotions, I kept my eyes closed, remaining a continent unto myself where blood flowed freely. My borders now secured, my soul was permitted to wander freely in the splatterlands.

Refusing to break my trance, I listened as the door creaked open and as cautious footfalls slipped into the room. My visitors reeked of a new kind of rot. No one spoke.

I felt hands reach beneath my armpits and lift me to my feet. Someone tore my shirt open and ripped Floyd's pendant from my neck. I was led outside to where the van idled softly, its exhaust smelling of diesel fumes. Inside, the vehicle smelled sweetly of death. I was shoved onto the back bench, and I finally opened my eyes.

We drove into the dying light of the day, heading into the heart of the city. As silence prevailed, my eyes drank in the artificial lights. I marveled at the façade of civilization the city presented, even when the ever-present voices of beasts whispered beneath the veil of night.

Darkness had arrived when we reached the far side of the city. Our destination was an abandoned and weather-worn factory, whose cracked walls serenaded the moon with a song of decay. The chain link fence surrounding the structure was the only thing on the premises that didn't look to be a century old. I was led inside, through a dark hallway and into a vast room. The chamber was clogged with smoke from fires burning inside barrels positioned in the corners. They didn't supply much light, and the room seemed softly illuminated by unknown sources.

I stood as an aspirant among the initiates. Awestruck and relieved to finally be among others like myself, I watched the dark rites that were already underway.

A tangled pile of bodies lie in the center of room, engaged in orgiastic worship. They slid among themselves with great viscosity, coated in a fluid that resembled dirty motor oil. A ring of initiates surrounded them, chanting softly. One of the figures stepped forward and dropped a torch into the carnal pile. The bodies instantly caught fire, yet the writhing continued as they melted into a confused mass of meat. Not one of them screamed.

I became hypnotized by the constellation of lust and pain before me. I never felt as close to Leviathan as I did in that moment. My flesh tingled and my animal unconscious was liberated. I stood among the initiates a complete being.

The clockwork motion of the orgy slowed and then stopped as the flesh evolved into ash.

"Ashes to ashes..." I muttered under my breath.

The initiates then turned their backs to the embers, and I felt all eyes fall upon me. Hands began to grab me, and my clothes were ripped from my body. I was thrown naked to the floor.

I set my mind against the stirrings of a primitive fear rising within me. The initiates fell upon me like wild predators. Teeth gnashed and ripped at my flesh, and hands tore chunks of meat from my bones. Nerve endings screamed as skin stretched and ripped. Blood spilled from me in great torrents. The last thing I saw with my old eyes was the delirious, blood-stained faces of the others, my flesh hanging in shreds from their teeth.

My consciousness was lost to blackness. I floated in the void between stars, nestled in the barbed arms of the Dark God. From space, I could see the last remnants of my physical self disappear down the gullets of the carnivorous worshippers.

I was floating in bliss, the blessed agony of eternal Hell, my self dissolved.

But then, slowly, a flicker, and as consciousness returned, my body began to descend. I floated disincarnate, but I was back in the chamber. I saw the gore-saturated floor where my body once lay. The initiates milled around, seemingly entranced.

My own thoughts and desires were now alien to me. I felt nothing, but yet was aware of the presence of my animal brain. Hunger and lust still existed in this sphere of my consciousness. But these feelings were transformed into a higher spiritual truth by the grace of Leviathan. The animal within and the soul stood united in bloodlust.

One of the initiates, the woman from the van, knelt over the bloodstain and began to wretch violently. A great torrent of blood and chunks of flesh were ejected from her mouth. The vomit pooled on the floor as the others gathered around her. Soon, they were all retching and their combined offal became an undifferentiated mass of meat and bodily fluid. The mess began to reform itself into a familiar shape, the shape of my body. I felt my consciousness sucked downward.

My flesh accepted my soul back into its house. I was born again in regurgitation. I was a newborn coated in a placenta of vomit. My soul stretched out in my transformed skin, no belly button, only a tangle of scarred flesh. Serpents writhed within me.

* * *

I celebrated my initiation with the others, a gore-soaked bacchanalia that raged into the night. There were sacrifices, strange drugs were imbibed, and even stranger copulations took place.

At some point, I must have passed out. When I awoke I was alone in the large room. Sunlight crept in through the grimy windows, casting my surroundings in a fungal glow. The others must have scurried off as dawn approached. I was again alone.

Freedom coursed through my veins. I felt compelled to take to the road again, to proselytize violence to the world, to put my initiation into practice. I was a beast set free into the wilderness, not lost but liberated.

I lay on the bloody floor for some time until I was startled by the sound of a car horn honking outside. I jumped to my feet and rushed to the doorway, hoping to see the black van. Instead, a beat-up pickup was parked in front of the building with its engine running. The driver's side door opened, and Barbas stepped out.

"Nothing creates life like death..." he said.

"...and nothing tastes as glorious as torn flesh between your teeth," I finished.

"Did you find what you were seeking?"

"I did," I replied," I don't know how to thank you."

"Come with me and hunt. Together we will construct edifices of meat and bone...a viscera of worship to Leviathan" Barbas replied.

"Of course."

I started to open the passenger door when Barbas motioned for me to stop. He stepped to the back and opened the tailgate of the truck. The bed was filled with something he had covered with a tarp.

"Perhaps our journey should begin with you meditating," he said. He pulled back the tarp. The pickup held three dead bodies which had been used in worship. He nodded, and I slipped beneath and joined them. I heard the driver's side door slam shut and felt him slip the truck into gear.

The vibration of the road quickly lulled me into a meditative state. I felt the cold flesh all around me, but I was comforted once again by the warm, barbed embrace of Leviathan.

ABOUT THE AUTHOR
ALLEN GRIFFIN

Allen Griffin is both an author and a musician who lives in Indianapolis, Indiana.

Griffin plays bass for Profound Lore recording artists *Coffinworm*.

Griffin's dark fiction has appeared in *Innsmouth Magazine*, *Indiana Horror Anthology 2011*, *Indiana Horror Anthology 2012*, *The Mustache Factor* and other venues.

His short story exploring themes of the occult, "Every Soul is a Grimoire," will be published in *Ominous Realities: Collected Works of Dark Speculative Fiction* from Grey Matter Press.

THE DEFILED
CHRISTINE MORGAN

We struck with the speed and fury of Thor's own lightning, plunging the sleeping village into a nightmare of fire and blood.

Steel glinted as our blades slashed, swords and axes cleaving deep into screaming flesh. Flames roared as thatched roofs burned, fierce blazes leaping against the skies to rival the dawn.

A man rushed us, thick-bodied but strong in his rage. He swept a cudgel meant to crack my skull. I turned the blow with my shield and spitted him through the gullet.

I felt the edge grate against the bones of his neck. I heard his angry cry drown in a gurgle. The pumping, red wave of his life gushed over me, splashing hot and thick on my face. I tasted it. I wrenched the weapon from his throat and laughed as he fell dying at my feet.

This was not glorious battle. This was glorious butchery.

A stripling, perhaps the son of the man I'd just slain, leapt at me with a shoddy dagger. Its tip caught in my mail-coat and bent. I bashed the lad's jaw in with my iron shield-boss, and hamstrung him as he whirled in a spray of shattered teeth.

Bjartrik, who fought naked but for a bearskin tied 'round his waist, swatted a squalling babe from the arms of its mother and stomped its head, bursting the soft skull like a ripe fruit beneath his heel. The woman went for his eyes with her fingernails, but missed, clawing his forehead. He ignored the scratches as he ripped off her clothes and threw her to the ground.

Her breasts were fat and full, squirting when Bjartrik's huge hands squeezed them. He opened her legs with such force that a hip dislocated with a loud, wet pop, but it did not deter him in the slightest. Falling on her, he commenced to a vigorous raping, greedily chewing at her engorged nipples until they leaked blood as well as milk.

Sigfrod snatched up what tokens of wealth there were to be found, mere trinkets of copper and hammered bronze for the most part. Ormund strode after an injured man, prodding him with a spear-point, enjoying his suffering as he crawled through the mud, trailing his unraveling guts.

Valfinn lashed together a group of frightened, bewildered children that were young and healthy enough to be taken as slaves. Vighulf, his brother, dragged a kicking and struggling woman who'd sought refuge in a goat-shed. Tunni, my friend, found a full jug of ale. He took a hearty swig of it, then passed it to me.

"To the hall!" That was Hrutr, our war-leader, his voice raised in a bellowing shout.

We rallied and went on the run, up the slope of the low rise where the lord of this place had built himself a longhouse. If silver or good plunder was to be had, we'd find it hidden within.

The last few able-bodied men of the village gathered to make a stand there, at the hall's doors. We had chosen the time of our attack well, waiting until after the lord's grown sons and sworn warriors had ridden off to lend aid to a neighboring jarl. Those that remained were farmers and peasants; they wore no coats of mail or even of leather. Roused from their beds, they were lucky to have pulled on their boots and breeches. One brandished a wood-axe, without much conviction. The others held cudgels, clubs and other farm tools.

They were dead men, and they knew it.

We numbered eight. Our ninth, Ulthor, had lost the toss and been left behind to guard our ship.

Eight fierce Vikings—outlaws and sea-raiders. But for Bjartrik in his bearskin, we came armed and armored. We came ready to kill.

Dead men though they were, they stood their ground as we waded into them. Steel hewed through wood, through bone. My blade pierced a man's chest, sinking between the ribs to skewer his heart. A head tumbled from a ragged, spouting neck-stump, and Tunni kicked it aside. Bjartrik caught the arm of a foe, snapping it across his knee like a length of kindling. Hrutr's longsword, well-seasoned and ever-thirsty, chopped one man nearly from shoulder to waist.

The last one, seeing the rest of his friends and kinsmen fall, tried making a run for it. Ormund and Valfinn gave chase, and it was no contest. Valfinn cut the fleeing peasant's legs from under him, spilling him to the ground. Then Ormund sprang upon him, sliced off the man's ears and made him eat them before he died.

From behind the doors came a sudden screaming.

We burst into a hall with hearth-pits down the center and sleeping-platforms lining the walls to both sides. The blankets, pelts and fleeces there were all in disarray, those who made them their beds having been roused from their slumber when we attacked.

The fires in the hearth-pits smoldered with the glow of banked embers, enough to show us a man whose trembling hands held a small, bloodied knife. He wore a night-tunic trimmed with squirrel-fur and a silver ring set with onyx and amber.

Tears streamed down his sallow cheeks into the grey of his beard.

A girl huddled before him, arms up and head down, long, golden hair hanging. A young girl, no doubt his daughter, and we knew at once what the old lord had done.

Hrutr strode toward her and yanked her head back, exposing her face. It must have been a fair face, even beautiful.

Now it was a horror.

The knife's work had well seen to that, cutting and carving. Her skin hung in flayed flaps. Her soft pink mouth had been shredded, her lips like rat-gnawed, raw meat. One blue eye stared shocked from the red-ruined mask. The other, punctured, oozed down her cheek like a broken egg. Had he meant to do that, to half-blind her? Or had his trembling hands slipped?

The rest of it, the disfiguring of her, had been no accident. Her father had done this with most deliberate purpose, to mar her fair beauty, to make her hideous, too ugly to rape.

"You cowardly pig's bastard!" Tunni drew back his sword.

"No!" Hrutr stayed him with a gesture, his gaze fixed on the old man. "Hold him."

Ormund and I did as he bade.

Then Hrutr seized the girl, spun her, and pushed her down on all fours with her face in the dirt and cold ashes by the hearth. He tore her shift from the hem to the waist, baring her unmarked nakedness.

We cheered our approval.

The lord thrashed, cursing, but could not hope to break free from Ormund's and my grasp.

The girl seemed too dazed to know what was happening as Hrutr hiked his mail coat and tunic, lowered his breeches, and knelt behind her. He spat in his palm and wetted his prick to thrust it home.

At that, she revived with an agonized shriek. Her father echoed it with a hoarse cry of despair.

"How is she?" asked Bjartrik, his grin wolfish.

"Tight as a miser with money," Hrutr said, ramming in again.

His fingers dug bruises into her hips. He fucked harder and harder, pounding away with a loud, meaty slapping of bodies. Howling, the girl scrabbled uselessly at the hearth-stones. When Hrutr finished with her, he patted her jovially on the rump and rose, adjusting his garments, leaving her sobbing on the floor.

Sigfrod took his turn next, followed by Tunni and Valfinn. By the time they were done, the poor girl lay sprawled on her muti-lated face with her arms splayed out to her sides. If not for some twitches and quivers, and a tortured whimpering, she might have been dead. Blood and spent seed coated her thighs in great crim-son streaks.

Her father, the lord, had no fight left in him. He sagged, weep-ing. He'd been able to shut his eyes to the scene, but not his ears.

Vighulf, who still had his captive—she looked terrified, and rightly so, as if she might be in for a similar fate—declined. So did I, for I preferred my women both plumper and less used.

When Bjartrik stepped up, more than ready again despite his recent ravishing of the milk-mother outside, cruel Ormund decided that this act most of all was one the lord needed to see. It needed three knuckles' worth of fingers chopped off before, begging for mercy, he could be made to look.

Bjartrik was a huge man in every regard, huge and hairy, his prick of a length and swollen girth all other men could but envy. Watching him position himself behind the girl was like watching a horse mount a doe. She only shuddered and made plaintive hurt-animal noises as he raped her, and fell senseless long before he reached his grunting conclusion.

Tunni joined me to permit Ormund a chance at the girl, though by then her father had lost any will or spirit he'd had left.

"Tight as a miser with money, didn't you say?" Ormund asked Hrutr. "Loose as a mud puddle now, I'd think. But this nether pucker is still snug and untouched." He spread the girl's buttocks and, without bothering to wet his prick first, drove it in to the hilt. She shrieked again as the shock of sudden pain revived her.

As Ormund subjected the girl to a thorough ass-fucking, the others set about looting the hall. They found a small sack of silver, a few brooches and pins, and a bronze circlet that the lord might have worn on his brow. Tunni pulled the ring from the lord's finger—one of those that had not been severed. He tossed it to Hrutr.

"Shall we kill him now?" I asked, looking down at the broken old man.

"Let him live," Hrutr said, as if magnanimous. "Perhaps we've given him a fine grandchild to remember us by."

"Bring him here, first," said Ormund, beckoning us forward.

We hauled him over. He found enough feeble strength to try to resist, but could not. Ormund seized him by the nape of his neck and pushed his face against the bloody, brutalized, shit-smeared swamp-hole of his daughter's loins. The mess painted him ear to ear and hairline to chin, his grey beard matted and sodden.

"Enough," said Hrutr. "Leave him, leave them. Let's go and be done and gone from this place."

Dawn's bright promise had been a lie; the foggy damp of morning was the truth. A sea-smell rode heavy in the air, portending rain.

The survivors we hadn't taken prisoner had fled. We stripped the dead of their meager valuables and searched the village for more. In one of the houses that had escaped unburned, a man had killed his wife and three children, then himself.

In another, I found a woman whose attempt at taking her own life had not gone as well as intended, or she'd too late had a change of heart. A length of twine, looped over the roof-beam, cinched her neck so that her face was puffing and purple.

But the cord was too long, so that her toes still touched the hut's hard-packed earth floor. Her fingers groped at the twine while her calves and ankles strained in a desperate effort to bear some of her weight from the noose.

She was a well-made figure of a woman, I saw. Plump-hipped and heavy-breasted.

Her eyes rolled and fixed frantically upon me. They flooded with an expression either imploring or relieved. As if I would save her and life as a captive was preferable after all, or I would grant her a swifter end than this slow strangulation.

Instead, I raped her. I raped her as she hung there. My thrusts alternately lifted her enough to let her gasp a half-breath, then lowered her so it was choked off again. When her thighs gripped my waist, I first thought she did it for leverage, to raise herself up and ease the noose's pressure. But, oddly, I also felt her begin to moisten, her inner tissues clasping wetly at my prick.

I ceased my thrusting and stood motionless, still buried within her. I stared, fascinated, into her eyes. Her mad, dying eyes—yet she writhed and squirmed, she ground her lower body against me like a lover, each sporadic breath a thin whistle in her throat.

The combined convulsions of ecstasy and death quaked within her simultaneously, even as I released my seed. I disengaged and backed away. She dangled there, limp now, lifeless, tongue protruding from her slack lips.

The house offered no other wealth but a whalebone comb and a bracelet of colored glass beads. I had just tucked these into the leather pouch I wore at my belt when I heard Vighulf's shout of alarm.

I rushed outside, as did the others, and we met up in the muddy lane between the huts.

Vighulf shouted again, pointing.

We looked toward the coast, toward the sea-inlet where we'd beached our small ship. Ulthor had stayed to protect it, with the understanding that what plunder we found would be evenly shared.

But Ulthor's body now lay sprawled upon the wet sand, unmoving and pierced by the gull-fletched shafts of many arrows. He must have been running to warn us when they shot him down in his tracks.

Another ship glided toward shore. A longship, a warship, far larger than ours, its striped sail rode furled, oars dipping and rising in graceful unison. What little daylight came through the lowering clouds glittered on helms and mail-coats, on sharp spear-points.

There were many men.

Dozens of them.

As many as thirty or more.

Armed men, warriors, and they greatly outnumbered us.

Even as we stared, aghast and astonished, their archers drew back on their bows. Another man touched a brand to each arrow's tip, setting ablaze wads of oil-soaked cloth. Then the archers let fly.

The flaming arrows flew true. They rained down upon our ship, to consume it with fire.

For a moment, none of us moved or spoke.

Then Hrutr said, "Follow me, and be quick if you cherish your lives!"

We followed. We were quick. All but the captive children, whom Valfinn had lashed together, thinking to sell them as slaves. They'd slow us so he cut them loose and set them running with slaps across their rumps. They scattered, wailing.

"What of her?" Vighulf asked. He had the woman's wrists leashed by a cord to his belt. She was tall and lean, coltish in the way Vighulf liked them, and those long, wiry legs suggested she'd well be able to keep up.

"Bring her," said Hrutr. "She knows the land." Pausing, he narrowed his eyes at her. "And she won't be foolish."

"Not if she knows what's good for her," Ormund said.

She went ashen, and gave an earnest nod.

So we went, out of the village, away from the huts and the hall, away from the blood-drenched corpses and the pyres where we'd torched the thatch. We went through field-lands and graze-lands.

We went ahead of the clamor of outrage and fury when the men from the ship beheld the carnage we'd left in our wake.

Not all would pursue us. There was that much, at least. They'd not leave their warship or the remains of the village undefended.

But some did give chase as we made for the woods. They had archers, fleet-footed and unencumbered, who wounded Sigfrod and shot down Valfinn and Tunni before we reached the shelter of the tree line.

We ran.

We hated to do it. We did not want to run, to leave our own dead behind. To leave them unavenged, their bodies unburned and unburied, in the hands of our enemies.

But we had to.

* * *

We left a trail a blind man couldn't have overlooked. Speed, rather than stealth, was our utmost intention.

Finally, we could run no further and had to stop to catch our breath. We looked at each other, stunned with shock, loss and shame. Vighulf, grief-stricken, embraced the woman and set his face to her neck and wept.

"See to Sigfrod's wounds," Hrutr said.

Ormund and I did. Sigfrod was in a bad way, the leg of his breeches dark with blood. An arrow's shaft had broken off, leaving the arrowhead embedded. We dug it out with a knife-point as he bit on a strip of leather.

While we rested, and Bjartrik kept watch, Hrutr questioned Vighulf's woman. Her name, she told us, was Jora. She was nineteen and unmarried, the man she'd been promised to having died last winter of a fever. We'd killed her father and uncle; she didn't know what had happened to the rest of her family.

"The next nearest village or hall?" Hrutr asked.

Jora gestured back the way we had come.

"And this way?"

"Woods," she said. "Woods, then the marsh."

Something changed in her voice. I glanced at her. We all did.

"The marsh?" I frowned. "What of it?"

"We don't go there."

"Why not?"

"The water is tainted," she said. "What grows there is poison and what lives there is worse. The marsh-folk—"

"Marsh-folk?" Hrutr leaned forward. "Do they have boats?"

"I...I think so, but—"

"Weapons?" Ormund interrupted.

She shrugged uneasily. "I heard that they hunt, and fish, but I've never been there. I've never seen them. They are dangerous."

"So are we," Bjartrik said, baring his teeth in that wolf's grin.

She went ashen again and shrank closer to Vighulf.

Vighulf, who'd had a hand in the deaths of her family, who had dragged her from hiding, captured and bound her, who she now turned to for comfort.

Women were strange.

Thunder rolled above the low clouds—Thor grumbling at the giants. The rain fell in fat, pattering drops.

We moved on without speaking, trudging through the damp,

dreary forest, growing weary and dispirited, hungry and irritable. Tempers shortened. Arguments arose.

We passed a wretched night, wrapped in our cloaks. Vighulf shared his with Jora but would not share Jora with us. For her part, the woman endured uncomplaining and with stoic acceptance.

The next day brought more rain and a dank, bone-deep chill. We fashioned Sigfrod a crutch from a forked tree-branch. Even so, he further slowed and hampered our progress.

"Where are we going?" Ormund eventually asked.

"She said the marsh-folk have boats," Hrutr replied. "They hunt and fish, so they must also have food. We'll take shelter there."

"You think they will help us?"

Hrutr jingled his belt-purse, then patted his sword. "With silver, or with steel, I think we'll convince them."

And so, we continued.

The land sloped downhill. The trees thinned and became spindly, while the underbrush sprawled in verdant profusion. The ground softened toward sponginess. Broad leaves dripped and puddles glimmered. Frogs croaked and splashed. We caught some and ate them, uncooked.

Then we came to a place where the mist-shrouded marsh spread out before us. It might have stretched forever, this muck and mire, this morass of grey, green and brown. Sluggish rills of water coursed through a maze of hummocks and scum-coated ponds. The air smelled of miasma and stagnation, making us grimace.

Hrutr chose the most promising of the meandering paths. We ventured after him into the marsh. A muffled hush descended around us. Within a few dozen paces, we could no longer see from where we had come. The twisting pathways and fog robbed even the best of us of our sense of direction.

We wondered about snakes. We worried about leeches. We slipped on slick swamp grasses and felt our feet sink in soggy holes. I took it into my head that the marsh-folk surrounded us, silent and unseen in the fog, keenly observing our every move with their flat and yellow eyes.

Why they would have flat and yellow eyes, I did not know. But the certainty was there in my mind.

The first one we saw was a grubby, club-footed youth wearing a coarse-spun shirt that was too large for him and fell to his bare, knobby knees. He had a line of fish over his shoulder. In his arms was a basket that slithered with eels. He regarded us with a dull, idiot's gape. His hair was stringy, his skin the color and texture of rancid tallow, his mouth wide and his chin nonexistent.

His eyes were not yellow, but I found them no less unsettling for it. They were of a muddy brown hue and...mismatched, somehow. As if one was larger than the other, and set crookedly in his face.

"Boy," Hrutr said. "You there."

The boy's wide mouth opened in a halfwit's grin. He chortled a hooting, doltish laugh. Though not deaf, he was possibly dumb, or addled. Maybe he did not understand our tongue. At last he seemed to understand what we wanted and beckoned us to follow into the fetid reaches of the marsh.

Cattails and lilies nodded on their stalks. We saw the quick flick of fish-tails and insects skating on the surface. There were tubby waterfowl, darting swift wings and long-necked, stick-legged birds of ugly disposition.

In some of the wider watercourses were wicker-weave traps for the catching of fish or eels. Here and there were larger land-rises where huts made of reeds and mud hunkered behind crude twig-fences. Some had what looked like gardens and pens for the keeping of animals. Thin tendrils of smoke wafted from chimney-holes and clay ovens.

The largest of these proved to be a cluster of hovels around a central work-area where fish were being cleaned and game were being dressed. For livestock, they had small, warty pigs and goats with scraggly wool. Dogs roamed about.

The other marsh-folk were much as the boy— grubby and disheveled, shabbily clothed, with such striking resemblances and deformities that we knew they must be of closer kin to one another than was healthy. Like the boy, they too did not speak our tongue. We saw no women, as if they'd secreted them away for safe-keeping at our approach, though there were some children.

Tired and hungry though we were, we could have overpowered them with ease. But, tired and hungry as we were, we didn't care to. Not when they gave us hospitable enough treatment, offering us food and drink and places to sit by the cook-fire.

The food was a watery stew of chopped fish, eel, and marsh-vegetables, but it was food, and it was hot, and we devoured it with great appetite. The drink proved less palatable, some sour concoction that wrinkled the nose. They showed us to a hut that had been vacated for our use. They brought us water to wash and an herb-poultice for Sigford's wound.

Hrutr repaid their kindness with a handful of copper and bronze trinkets from our plunder, which pleased them but did not visibly inspire them to greed or menace. It was as if they had little comprehension of value.

We were, however, not so confident and trusting as to fail to set watches while we slept.

* * *

I woke with a throbbing in my skull, a sickness in my stomach and a vile taste in my mouth. I woke to the sensation of moving on water. I woke to darkness, a close and stifling darkness. I woke to the sound of ripples lapping at a plank hull, and the dip and slosh of an oar-pole. And to the realization I was bound hand and foot with rough ropes, lying in the bottom of a boat, with a sack drawn over my head.

We had set watches.

Yet somehow they had gotten to us nonetheless.

Had they drugged us? Something in the fish stew? Not the drink. We'd barely touched it, so it must have been the stew.

I struggled, tugging at the bonds. I thrashed, pitching the small boat violently side to side. I knew I risked upending it, dumping myself into the water, but—

A hard blow cracked against my temple. I had time to think it was the butt-end of a stave or a spear, then nothing more.

* * *

I next woke to shouts and cursing.

I inhaled a mulchy stench and felt an unpleasant dampness beneath my body. I realized I was naked as a newborn.

My mail-coat, my sword, my helm and shield and axe were gone.

I opened my eyes to a sickly and sputtering firelight. It came from torches stuck into the black tops of rotting stumps. The light illuminated the interior of a fortress of sorts, a swamp stronghold where earthen embankments had been built up around a hollow and topped with a palisade of hewn logs. Within the hollow were more of the mud huts and hovels.

The others were there with me, all of us naked within an enclosure, guarded by marsh-folk armed with gaffs.

This did not bode well.

I sat up. My head ached.

The shouting and cursing came from my companions. Bjartrik taunted the guards, daring them to free and face him, challenging them to fight. Ormund swore threats and insults at them, dark imprecations of what he'd see done to them, how he'd see that they suffered.

The marsh-folk, if even they understood, made no reply. They seemed as malformed and strange as those we'd seen before, if not more so.

"Save your breath," Hrutr said. "Save your strength. We'll need both for when we get out of this."

They both grudgingly complied. Sigfrod remained unconscious from whatever drug we'd been given. Vighulf cast his gaze about, anxious and distraught.

"Where's Jora?" he asked. "What have they done with her?"

"Worry more for yourself, and for us," I told him.

He scowled and said nothing.

Three more men, not marsh-folk but strangers, watched from the rear corner of the enclosure. Two were grossly obese, wallowing on beds of woven grass mats piled with leaves. When we looked at them they turned away, their movements the ponderous effort of great, clumsy weight. Tattered, filth-caked blankets could not hide that they, too, were naked.

The third, thin and wiry, wore the grimy rags of a deerskin knotted around his scarred midsection like a robe. The cheerful smile of welcome he gave us was half-toothless and mad. It made us uneasy. He cackled. We ignored him.

More marsh-folk busied themselves at a low platform built of stacked branches. It resembled a smaller version of a funeral pyre, though the dank wood, with its slimy bark, looked far too wet to burn or even smolder.

"What's that for?" Vighulf put voice to the question in each of our minds, although it was a question we truly did not want answered. "Do they intend to make sacrifice of us?"

"That," said Ormund, "or butcher, cook and eat us."

The man in the ragged deerskin cackled again.

We glanced at him, but before any of us could decide to speak, more marsh-folk appeared. Though there still were no women among them, a few of their freakish children capered about like gnomes, and some of the men carried infants in slings against their backs or chests.

Then we did see a woman, not a marsh-woman, but someone we knew.

"Jora!" Vighulf threw himself at the fence and stuck his hands out toward her. "Have they harmed you?"

She hesitated, then approached. In all my days I had never seen a look so cold. "No," she said. "They have not."

"Oh, they wouldn't have hurt her," said the cackling man in the knotted deerskin, who had joined us by the fence. "They do not abuse women. Oh, no. They don't dare."

Vighulf dropped his voice to a whisper. "You must help us."

"Why would I?" asked Jora.

"But—" He gaped at her.

"You attacked my home," she said, her tone that of explaining a simple truth to a simple child. "You killed my family, my friends!"

"I thought we...you and I..."

"You raped me!"

"I protected you!"

"From them!" She swept an angry gesture to encompass the rest of us. "Not from yourself. You raped me!"

"You...you didn't object!"

"Would it have stopped you?"

At that, Vighulf downcast his eyes.

Jora huffed a disdainful snort as she turned away.

"She told them, you see," said the deerskin-clad madman. "Told them all about you."

"But they don't speak our tongue," Hrutr said. "They don't understand us."

"Not all of them, no." He rocked back and forth from his toes to his heels, scratching at the great scar on his belly. It must have been a terrible wound, a gutting stroke many men would not have survived. "Some of them do. The crone does. And I understand theirs. A bit. Only a bit, you see. But enough."

"Crone?" Ormund and I echoed together.

He smiled half-toothlessly again. "I told you they do not abuse women, but they did once, ah yes! Or their fore-fathers did. Abused them until they'd nearly killed them off, mothers and sisters and baby daughters alike. Then came the plague-time, the curse-time.

She, the crone, was the only one left. They fear and revere her, and all women, now."

"And who in Hel's name are you?" asked Hrutr.

"Nafni," he said. "I was a trader. I tried to find a swift trade route through the marshlands. Pride and folly, you see. Stupid of me. Ran my ship aground on a mud bank and there they found us. Those two? The last of my men. Aolf and Fjodr."

"What happened to the others?" I asked.

"Oh, and here comes the crone herself," Nafni said. By the flicker in his mad eyes, he seemed glad of the interruption.

The hag was no more the pleasant to look upon than the rest of the marsh-folk. Her back was hunched, her feet not club-footed but bony and bent awkwardly outward so that she hobbled on their callused edges. One arm was a withered crook, the hand fused into two stubby fingers and the claw of a thumb. Above her mismatched yellow eyes was a lump of vein and gristle that almost resembled an off-center third eye.

A necklace of dried frogs and bird's heads rested against her flat, wrinkled breasts. Around her scrawny waist was a belt of braided cloth strips; a knife hung on one side and a pouch on the other.

Crone indeed, and no better word for it, I thought.

She squinted at us through the stakes of the fence. "You," she said to Hrutr. "You be Norske-man leader. You be first."

"If you're going to kill us," he replied, "give us weapons so we can fight like men."

"No kill. No fight, no kill. No good killed."

"What, then?"

"Norske-man be made with us."

It went on for a time, Hrutr trying with increasing exasperation to argue, bargain, reason with and intimidate the crone, but to no avail.

"Whatever it is," Ormund said, "it must be better than sitting here penned like pigs in our own shit."

Hrutr nodded.

The guards held their gaffs poised, keeping the rest of us at bay.

More marsh-men seized Hrutr as he stepped out. In a matter of moments, despite his resistance, they'd overpowered him. They dragged him to the platform of branches and slung him face-up atop it, tying his wrists over his head and his ankles to a post.

The crone, standing beside Hrutr, drew her knife.

Fresh terror washed over us.

"They're going to unman him!" Vighulf dropped his hands into his lap, cupping them to cover himself.

"I'd rather be butchered," Bjartrik said.

We all shared his sentiment and winced as the crone lowered the blade.

But the knife did not slice off Hrutr's prick, and it did not geld the sack of his stones.

It touched his stomach midway between navel and groin. The sharp tip indented the skin so that a single bead of blood welled up.

"Be still, Norske-man," the crone said. "Be still or much more the pain."

She made a small incision, a precise crescent-shaped cut.

We saw Hrutr's fists clench. We saw his jaw tighten and his body tense. We saw more blood well up from the line of the wound. The crone inspected her handiwork, then turned.

"Gipa?" she said, beckoning.

One of the marsh-men approached. This one was, of them all,

the most disfigured and hideous yet—slope-shouldered, bow-legged, his misshapen head bulging, his skewed mouth unable to fully close so that his tongue hung out, drooling.

He climbed the branches like ladder-rungs to the top of the platform. He straddled Hrutr, standing over his hips. Peeling aside his loincloth, he released a gnarled and jutting grotesqueness.

I understood, then. So did Ormund. The others remained baffled in their dread and revulsion, until the marsh-man hunkered down, crouching, and brought the knobby end of his prick to nudge at the opening cut into Hrutr's belly.

Now, they understood. We all did, though we did not want to believe. It left us dumb-struck and mind-numbed, this horror all but beyond comprehension.

Hrutr screamed like a raped virgin when the prick slid inside him. Which, in this sense, I suppose that he was. More blood flowed, dribbling down his sides.

"Be still," advised the crone again. "Gipa do slow. Gipa do gentle."

The marsh-man eased his prick deeper with a careful, flexing push of his buttocks. Hrutr screamed again.

"Uuuhhr," Gipa sighed. He smacked his lips.

"It's the bowels, you see," Nafni said. "The entrails, the intestines. They don't want to rupture those. And they..." He laughed, a madman's light and carefree laugh. "They like the way it feels. Slippery, you see. Warm and wet and slippery. Like a jarful of warm, squirming worms. Much better than a cunt or an ass or a mouth, they say."

"They'll have to kill me first!" said Bjartrik, and the rest of us gave vehement agreement.

Nafni tutted. "They don't want to do that."

Gipa grasped Hrutr's hipbones and quickened the pace of his thrusts. He groaned and slobbered. His pendulous sack bounced against Hrutr's groin. Hrutr no longer screamed like a virgin but sobbed like one, a helpless and terrible sound.

Even more terrible was the sound of this unspeakable gut-fucking, the thick and slopping slosh of curdled butter being churned.

"Uuhr...uhhhhhr..." Gipa panted. His haunches humped with the rapid urgency of a dog on a bitch. "Uh! Uh! Urrrrrgh! Hahhhhh...ahh...hnn..." Exhaling a satisfied gusty breath, he settled his buttocks onto Hrutr's thighs.

He withdrew his prick in a glut of blood, slime and other fluids too disgusting to contemplate. This, he wiped off on Hrutr's crotch-hair. He then clambered off, readjusting his loincloth.

Hrutr just lay there, eyes squeezed shut with tears trickling at their corners. His fists remained clenched, white-knuckled.

The crone patted his shoulder. "Good, big, brave Norske-man," she said in a tone of cloying condescension. "Not so bad, no?"

She washed the wound with a rag dunked in a bucket of water. The incision had torn at the edges. It looked gouged, bruised and inflamed. Hrutr still did not move. His chest shuddered as it rose and fell.

"This little more now," the crone told him, and began stitching the raw, reddened flesh closed with a thick, dark thread.

When she was done sewing, she had the marsh-folk untie him. They helped him up and led him back to the enclosure, where we remained too aghast to speak or move. Hrutr took careful, mincing paces as if it hurt him to walk. More tears trickled helplessly down his face, which contorted in an agony of pain and humiliation. I reached out a hand to him and he slapped it furiously away. He flinched from our gazes and would not look at us. He went to the furthest space in the pen that he could find. There, he lowered himself to the ground—curled up—and lay shaking.

They took Sigfrod next. He, having only barely begun to regain consciousness, could make only the most fitful resistance as they secured him and the crone's knife sliced its crescent-shaped cut.

"Leave him alone!" cried Vighulf. "He's injured already!"

"Oh, that's why, you see," Nafni said. "He's injured already. He might not live. So, there's less to lose letting one of the young ones have at him."

"Young ones—?" Bjartrik started to ask, then saw Gipa leading another of the marsh-folk toward the platform.

It was the youth, the boy, the one who'd met us in the swamp and led us to his village.

"You frog-lipped, frog-sucking little bastard!" Ormund shouted.

The boy jumped, but the crone soothed him.

"It's an honor for him, you see," Nafni went on. "His reward."

Sigfrod—confused, drug-addled—did not seem to know what was going on as the youth climbed up and squatted astride him.

The youth shucked off his long shirt. His prick curved up from his loins. He blushed when the crone inspected it, then grinned, tongue-lolling when she stroked it approvingly. She gurgled and muttered to him in whatever language these people spoke. He nodded, his crooked eyes all but dancing in anticipation.

The crone took hold and guided the boy into the incision.

With an ear-splitting shriek, Sigfrod woke fully. He lifted his head and looked down to see what was being pulled back out of the bleeding hole in his belly.

Unlike Gipa, but like any over-eager lad, the youth could not 'do slow' or 'do gentle.' He plunged it in again, pushing hard and fast, making bestial, gobbling grunts.

Sigfrod shrieked and shrieked. The more he struggled, the more excited the boy became, the harder and faster his plunging thrusts.

If the sounds had been terrible before, they were a hundred times worse now, a squelching and popping like decaying kelp pods bursting under running boots. Then Sigfrod's shrieks hit a height no man's throat should have been able, and the stink of shit suddenly flooded the air. Brown fluid and bile squirted out, along with the blood.

"You see?" Nafni said, still rocking toe-to-heel, fingers laced behind him. "Ruptured his bowels. Happens with the young ones. They're not careful enough."

The youth, spent, collapsed onto Sigfrod.

Who was, we saw, dead, and we could only find it a mercy.

Other marsh-men surrounded the boy, helping him down, clapping his back in what must have been congratulation. Some of them spoke to him in the marsh-tongue, the tone suggesting praise, advice and jovial teasing.

They dumped Sigfrod's body ignominiously for the dogs.

And then they came for Vighulf.

"This Norske-man?" the crone asked of Jora.

"Yes," she said. All this while, through the unnatural proceedings, she'd stayed by the crone, as attentive as an apprentice at the elbow of the master. Was it not enough for her that she'd been spared from further defilement? Why would she choose this marsh-life, these strange marsh-ways? Had she, like Nafni, gone mad?

"Jora!" Vighulf called to her, imploring.

"You raped me," she told him again.

"We could be married!"

She spat in his face.

Jora had been, I recalled, stoic and enduring. Vighulf was neither. Vighulf wept and begged when the crone sliced his belly, wailed like a lamb at the slaughter when one of the marsh-folk mounted him, and wept again when Jora, under the crone's tutelage, stitched him up. She did seem mad, I thought. The reverence of the marsh-folk and the encouragement of the crone must have begun that, and the revenge upon Vighulf completed it.

Through it all, Hrutr did not move from where he curled shaking on the ground. He did not move when Vighulf was brought back, still weeping, hobbling in that same pained manner. Nor did he move when the crone beckoned to Bjartrik, or when Bjartrik lashed out at those who attempted to seize him.

He caught hold of two and cracked their skulls together with such force that both marsh-men were instantly killed. Roaring his battle-cry, he picked up another and hurled him through the air.

Ormund and I also leapt to attack. Naked, unarmed and outnumbered, we flung ourselves into the fray.

A barbed, wooden fish-spear caught Ormund in the backside and ripped him open. He fell dying, screaming, writhing in blood and shit. As for Bjartrik and me, they beat us down. Crushing us into the mud, battered and broken.

Darkness fell over me. I hoped it was death.

* * *

"Well, you brought that upon yourselves, you see," I heard a voice saying.

Nafni's voice.

The darkness that had fallen over me wasn't death after all.

I opened my eyes, or at least as far as they would open.

"I'm alive?" I asked in a groan.

"They spared you."

Everything hurt. I could not even begin to take a tally. I was back in the enclosure. I felt as if I'd been trampled by iron-shod horses, or wrung like a rag in the fists of a stone giant.

I turned my head and saw Hrutr and Vighulf, or the backs of them, curled into their shuddering misery as they were. I did not see Ormund, and supposed his corpse was by now with Sigfrod's, among the scavenging dogs.

I turned my head the other way and saw through the stake fence that they had Bjartrik upon the platform with three slits cut into him—one below the navel and another above each hip—and while one marsh-man gut-fucked him from the top, two others did the same from each side.

They were not the first, judging by the sludge of blood and seed that seemed to cover Bjartrik from chest to thigh. Nor were they to be the last, judging by the way more marsh-men stood waiting.

"He, however," Nafni said, "well, he slew several of the folk, so it was decided their kinsmen should each have a turn. Still, he is a large man, strong and healthy, and he might survive."

"Why? Why not kill us?"

"Oh, they need you."

Just then, a frightened and wavering call came from the enclosure's far corner, where the last men from his trade ship wallowed on their beds of leaves and woven grass. Aolf called again, pleading. "Nafni? Nafni!"

"You'll be fine," Nafni said to me. "You're a strong and healthy man, too. You'll be fine. You'll see."

He left to answer that plaintive call. I tried to sit up, but when I did, such a clenching wave of agony wrenched through me that I almost vomited. I fell back, shivering, covered in a clammy and nauseous sweat.

I remembered.

No.

I remembered nothing. The fight, and they beat us down, and then nothing.

I did not remember anything else.

I was determined not to remember anything else.

The thin, stinging slice of the crone's blade, for instance.

Or the gross invasion of—

No!

The slick and sinking press, the sundering thrusts—

No!

A deep, bruising, relentless pain worse than any gut-cramps I'd ever experienced—

I touched my midsection and the agony flared again, the way a coal might flare from banked embers to white-hot at a breath of air. My fingertips probed gingerly downward until they found what...

What I had known...

But did not and would not remember...

The loathsome, living meatiness of it...

Which I would not let myself remember...

The coarse thread made a line of stitches along the incision below my navel. A congealing stickiness seeped through. The skin
felt puffy and sore.

I closed my eyes, struggling against that urge to vomit. If I did,
the heaving and retching would rip me apart.

Nafni signaled for the crone and she hurried over, quick on her
out-bent feet, to where Aolf wallowed on his mat. They conferred,
then she raised her voice in a spate of orders to the marsh-folk.
Several came bustling into the enclosure. A mood of anxious expectation filled the air. I was reminded of something, but could not
right away think of what.

Even Hrutr and Vighulf turned, craning their necks to see what
the commotion was about.

If ever we had a chance to try and make our escape, this surely
was it, but the act alone of sitting up brought new spasms of pain
to my violated innards. I could not imagine having to stand or
walk or run or fight.

From where I lay, I could see the stricken Aolf more clearly than
I wanted to. His tattered blanket had fallen off, revealing not the
jiggling fatty folds of obesity after all but a great, gravid dome.

It was not possible.

It could not be.

The skin rippled and bulged as if something moved just beneath
it. There was the momentary but all-too-vivid impression of a foot,
a hand, the rounded bump of a head.

I remembered now what I had been reminded of before. The
marsh-folk, the way they clustered around the crone like village
women to a midwife...

Aolf convulsed, heels drumming the earth. His face knotted

with strain. The noises he made were like those of someone in the throes of both labor and constipation. Nafni mopped at his brow with a muddy rag.

Low on the undercurve of his belly was a line of scar, a healed-over incision. The crone, with that same small, trusty knife, sliced into it. She extended the cut in a long, sweeping arc. Blood loosed in a river.

She reached into the belly. She dug about, groping, elbows-deep. The sounds were wet and ghastly. Aolf shrieked again, louder than ever.

Finally, red-drenched halfway to the shoulders, the crone drew a squirming thing from this grisly mess. She held it high. Chubby arms and legs waved. The marsh-folk uttered hooting, glad cheers. She handed it off to Nafni. He inspected it closely.

"A boy," Nafni told Aolf, who lay gurgling with sobs. "It's a boy, a fine sturdy boy! Hardly a blemish or deformity at all!"

This did not much seem to comfort or assuage him.

Try though the crone did to re-pack the guts and stitch the incision shut again, he resisted her efforts. He fought for his own death. And, when his entrails gushed out, disemboweled in a glut, he won the battle.

The other man, Fjodr, began screaming then, beating with his fists at his own distended and impregnated belly. He was swiftly subdued and bound so that he could not harm himself or that which grew within him.

The newborn had been handed over to one of the marsh-folk who held it to his chest where it latched onto a warty nipple like a calf at the udder and began hungrily suckling. Others crowded around, eager to have a look at the child.

"Mine was stillborn," Nafni said. He rubbed his scar, and sighed. "The poor little babe. Perhaps the gods never meant for me to have sons."

Aolf's corpse was taken away. They finished with Bjartrik, had Jora sew his wounds, then returned him, unconscious but still clinging to life and breath, to the enclosure.

Food was thrown to us, and blankets, and woven grass mats.

The marsh-folk went to their huts. Jora followed the crone.

Then it was quiet.

The torches burned low.

We were left alone with our thoughts and our pain.

"They need you," Nafni had said.

The marsh-folk, in all their deformity and strangeness.

"*The water's tainted,*" Jora had said. "*What grows there is poison and what lives there is worse.*"

"*The plague-time, the curse-time,*" Nafni had told us.

"*Norske-man be made with us,*" the crone had said.

I looked at Vighulf and Hrutr, who stared back at me with blank and empty madness in their eyes.

I looked at Nafni, his midsection a knotwork of scars. And gravid Fjodr, bound and weeping while the thing within him stirred.

They needed us.

And now we knew why.

ABOUT THE AUTHOR
CHRISTINE MORGAN

Christine Morgan works the overnight shift in a psychiatric facility and divides her writing time among many genres.

A lifelong reader, Morgan also writes, reviews, beta-reads, occasionally edits and dabbles in self-publishing. She has several novels in print, with more planned and due out soon. Her stories have appeared in more than two dozen anthologies, magazines and e-chapbooks.

Morgan has been nominated for the Origins Award and received Honorable Mentions for her work in two volumes of *Year's Best Fantasy and Horror*.

She's also a wife, mom and possible future crazy-cat-lady whose other interests include gaming, history, superheroes, crafts and cheesy disaster movies.

THE ARTIST
JAMES S. DORR

Art: The quality or expression or performance
of that which is pleasing to the senses;
that which is raised to more than ordinary importance.
Artist: One who produces art.

Is art permanent? I seem to remember they said that in school, but what about music? I mean, I know there are records and tapes now, but what about before those things were invented? Would an original performance conducted by Beethoven be any less art because it hadn't been taped? Or an opera by Verdi be called commonplace simply because it hadn't been filmed?

Some say art deals with the unexpected. A couple of senators— you know, in Washington—say it's obscene. I say it's beauty.

Just that: beauty. It takes in the rest.

The unexpected? The discovery of beauty in that which is plain. The *found* importance.

My wife doesn't understand art.

* * *

Sarah, my wife, had a thing for uniforms ever since before we were married. For marching men.

"Vince," she would say, "why don't we plan to go out and watch the parade tomorrow? See the K of C with their flags and swords?"

Columbus Day, sure. "You know I work holidays," I'd reply. "Got a banquet tomorrow night. But I'll tell you what, Sarah. Why don't you go? You can tell me all about it."

"Sure, Vince," she'd say. Sometimes she'd call me 'Vinnie.'

"But don't forget, Sarah, to get back in time. We got to get dressed, right?"

"Sure, Vince," she'd say. Then she'd go back to watching TV, or whatever else it was she was doing. She'd watch for an hour, maybe two hours, then turn and look at me.

"Vince," she'd say, "why don't *you* join the Knights of Columbus? Really get dressed up, you know, with the blue and gold..."

"Sarah, Sarah, Sarah," I'd say. I'd take her into my arms and I'd kiss her. "Sarah," I'd say, "you know I don't have time to march in parades. I've got to create."

She'd nod and kiss me back. She'd mutter, "Yeah, I know, Vince. You're a good butcher. You're good to me, too."

She'd go back to watching her show on TV and I'd think. *A good butcher?* I'd wonder, *That's all she thinks of me? Of what I do?*

Like Michelangelo was a craftsman, or Frank Lloyd Wright, maybe, had a job in the construction business? But then I'd look at her and I'd see she'd been crying a little. So I'd go to her and kiss her again.

"Maybe someday," I'd say, and I'd hug her. "Maybe someday when I have my own apprentice. I understand at the K of C lodge you can get drinks cheap."

"Yeah, Vinnie," she'd say. "I understand that, too." She'd laugh and be happy and I'd remember, all over again, why I loved her so much, even if she *didn't* understand art.

* * *

Does art understand art?

That is, can an object embody a virtue and know of its qualities at the same time? An interesting question, but one I haven't had the education to answer.

My education: grammar school and high school. The old *eight-four* system. Six years apprenticed to Marcino's Fancy Groceries. Married to Sarah, a non-Italian girl I met at a dance—my inspiration. That's when I discovered meat as an art.

You know what I mean? You've heard of ice carvers. Sometimes they get mentioned in the newspapers, at winter carnivals, things like that. Openings of ski lifts. They take a big block of ice, sculpt a lion, maybe a soldier or a knight in armor. Sometimes a dragon. It gets on TV.

And then there are soft molders, artists in things like butter and cheese who make centerpieces for fancy dinners. What I do is a kind of a combination.

I sculpt in ground meat. Mr. Marcino started me off.

"Vinnie," he said, "we got a policemen's banquet we got to cater tomorrow and now the chief calls me. Says he wants to have sixteen hamburgers, shaped like little guns or something, to give to the mayor and the council. Something special, but I ain't got time. You think you can take it?"

I thought of Sarah. We'd just been married. I thought of how proud she would be if I could, especially since we'd get tickets to go to the banquet ourselves so I could attend to the final details.

"Sure," I answered.

I worked all that night—called Sarah to tell her I wouldn't be home. That night I discovered the method that has since become sort of my trademark—a combination of molding and sculpting. I ground the steak five times to make it fine, then formed it by hand into the shape of the pistols. Then I flash froze it, leaving it malleable in the center, but hard on the surface. Then, with an ice pick—now I use chisels, just like a stone sculptor—I carved the details: grooves on the cylinders, little cross hatchings on each butt. I used a pencil to push in the bores and the little holes that define the chambers.

The work was pretty crude by the standards I hold to today, but the thing is, the mayor loved it. I understand he still keeps his at home in his freezer.

And when Marcino's finally closed down, it was the mayor who got me banquet work as a freelancer.

* * *

I looked Sarah up once. The name, I mean, in the big dictionary we keep on the shelf behind the TV.

Sarah means "princess."

And then I wonder, does even a princess know what it means to be a princess?

* * *

Those days were hard on both me and Sarah. The fancy grocery and meat-to-order trade had been killed by the supermarkets. I bought a used freezer, a big lean-in model, and set it in the back pantry at home, and I got a deal on Marcino's own grinder. It helped us get by.

I did Democratic Party picnics—nothing *real* fancy but, with the mayor's help, I made more contacts.

And then it turned around. People, all of a sudden, had money. They still liked the supermarkets' convenience, but, especially when they gave dinners, they started to want things a little nicer.

And banquets came back. Republicans, this time, but that didn't matter.

October 12, Columbus Day morning, I kissed my princess—my Sarah—goodbye and walked to the Eighth Street Supermarket where, under Tony Lagaducci, I run the custom meat department. Now Lagaducci himself is no artist. He's the head butcher for the store, while Mr. Wagman is the chain's manager. Lagaducci and I get along, though. We sort of have to.

For instance, this time my work involved a major sculpture. A big Spanish galleon, just like Columbus had, made out of meat. For something this big, we borrowed back and forth.

That is, we pool our meat orders to start with, for sake of the price. But different meats have different uses for someone like me.

In this case, coarsely ground beef formed the hull, while pork was shredded in twine-like frozen links for the rigging. But central to the work was the great expanse of sails, fashioned from veal, white from the grinder and molded in curved sheets that, when surface frozen, formed a canvas for red food-dye crosses and golden sunbursts. The magical signs that accompanied Columbus across the sea.

You see what I mean? Now, veal is expensive and, normally, one doesn't order much. And for something like this there's a lot of wastage. Yet few other meats can match its shiny, fine-colored surface, its smoothness of texture. So that's when I borrow.

With Lagaducci's permission, of course, some of it goes onto his account, with this understanding: when I'm finished I'll re-grind the waste meat into patties, wrap them in cellophane into packets and put them on sale on the regular meat shelves. This way, generally, he'll get back more than his part of the order accounts for, so we adjust again. This time, maybe, he gives me back liver—something I don't order for myself much because people don't like it. But liver is black and good for detail work, like, in this case, the ship's little cannon.

Mr. Wagman doesn't approve of this, but it works out. Lagaducci and I don't approve of each other either—we *do* get along—but when I'm between commissions, I help him with the regular meat cutting, just as he helps me on days like today by lending me an apprentice or two.

It gives me a chance to turn on the TV across from the freezer and watch a little bit of the parade. To wonder if Sarah is out there watching.

And that's when I saw her.

She rushed from the crowd—her thing about uniforms. She rushed right up and kissed a cop in one of the precinct marching units. Right there on TV.

Blue and gold all around her.

* * *

Policemen wear blue-and-gold uniforms too. Like the Knights of Columbus. Blue and gold follows me.

Like my first dinner—the little revolvers.

The idea was the head table guests had these plastic bullets. Red was for rare, blue for medium, yellow for well done, and they'd put one on their plates with their carved, ground-beef guns, indicating how they wanted their meat cooked. Waiters took the plates back to the kitchen, put the revolvers into broilers that cooked them in minutes, then took them out smoking, with buns and condiments heaped on one side, just the way their owners had ordered.

After that more work came my way. And with it, I was able to start to perfect my art. For instance, the annual Christmas Boar's Head—something I now do for free as a charity for St. Boniface Seminary—became the first sculpture in which I combined different kinds of meat.

The bulk of that first head, as might be expected, was made from ground pork, but ground in a lumpy, gnarled sort of way. The eyes were just black-dyed, but deeply set so it didn't matter. But for the apple—the bright, red apple to go in the boar's mouth—no matter how many times I ground it, pork just wouldn't do.

That's when I first discovered veal. Just for detail work, like apples and tusks, since it *was* expensive. But nothing else gave the fineness of surface, the natural pale lustre, the ability to take color as well when color was needed.

* * *

And then I discovered there was one other flesh that could be used as well.

Oh, yes. I admit it. That second Christmas, the hardest winter of the recession we had gone through back then, I couldn't find veal. Not that I could've afforded it either. But never mind that, the shops didn't have it.

I tried to use turkey, for its color, but that was a failure. Even then I was too much of an artist to accept its crumbly quality, its way of flaking instead of acquiring the sheen of trapped ice when it started to soften.

I tried other meats. I even thought of cheese as a substitute— I'm not ashamed to admit what I went through.

I prayed for a miracle. Sarah and I *needed* the commission.

And God interceded. God understands artists. I think if anyone could be said to be God's partner, it must be the artist. His fellow creator.

God sent the vagrant who froze to death in the alley behind my house. Sarah was still in bed that morning when I went out.

When I got the idea.

I just needed one arm. I wrapped the rest of the body and hid it in the big lean-in freezer. I carved flesh from bone—the bone I disposed of—and used the grinder Marcino had sold me. I ground it up fine. Right there in the kitchen.

I had already half-colored the apple by the time Sarah came down to fix breakfast.

* * *

These days there's no need for substitutions. After all, I have the run of the whole meat section, what with borrowing and pooling orders. But, back in those days, I'll admit it. That wasn't the only time I went to humans.

You see, I came to realize that for some purposes—times when I need even more exquisite surface detail—human flesh can be better. It grinds more cleanly—even than veal—and, under ideal circumstances, it will retain somewhat of its texture when well past the point of thawing.

And even after times became better, for major commissions I still sought out humans. Prostitutes, derelicts, bums on the street—those who would never be missed in the commonplace world—became parts of my sculpture. Became, as it were, art. And afterwards, yes, were sometimes eaten.

The boars' heads were always just decorations for Christmas Eve, but on Christmas Day they were re-ground and baked into small meat pastries to be given out to the city's poor. And no one complained, because who would notice? Sometimes, though she didn't know it herself, Sarah used some of my human scraps to make our own dinners. Again, how could anyone tell?

Even the well-to-do rarely eat veal, except when they sometimes find it on sale. And even then, when it's ground into patties, it's cooked with sauces that hide the flavor.

Chemical analysis? Yes, that would show a difference. If the police should come to suspect me, should come to miss, shall I say, one of my victims, I dare say they'd find me out quickly enough. But I and Sarah and the police got along well together.

* * *

Columbus Day evening Sarah called to beg off joining me at the banquet.

"I watched the parade. It was really good, Vinnie, except it was too long. I'm home now, but tired, so would you mind awfully much if I just had a bite to eat here and went to bed early?"

"I know," I said. "About the parade. I saw you on TV. When the police post was marching by."

There was a short silence, then a chuckle. "Oh, Vinnie," she said. "Then maybe you saw me with Officer Collins. I don't know what came over me then, except that maybe he's such a nice man. You know him too, Vinnie, from some of the functions? He moonlights as a security guard."

Yes, then I placed him. Patrolman Second Class Peter Collins. He often worked banquets where my art was featured, and like Sarah said, he always went out of his way to be pleasant. I let Sarah go, then wondered if I saw him that night if I should mention he'd been on TV.

But I didn't see him.

* * *

After Columbus Day the banquet circuit starts in earnest. Thanksgiving turkeys are ground and remolded, left hollow inside to be stuffed with individually wrapped sausages and cheeses. At Christmas, as always, there's the traditional Boar's Head Dinner. The work becomes so much that Sarah and I often find ourselves growing distant during the holiday season.

And then this year, in February, I was offered the Cattlemen's Banquet. This was to be a Western-styled dinner with, as its focus, a life-sized sculpture of a Black Angus bull done entirely in ground steak. You might think this was a simple commission—just one kind of meat—except that the restaurant owners who sponsored it wanted a different kind of detail than the sort I was used to.

For this work of art, different grades of beef were to correspond with the parts they were originally carved from. Does that make sense? For instance, rump was to be used for the bull's rear; sirloin, then short loin, then rib for its sides; brisket and chuck for its forward portions; even ground tongue. In a way it was funny.

An artistic joke.

And I loved the humor.

I spent long nights with Lagaducci, making out order forms together. Flank and plate, foreshank and chest floor. Meats that few people normally call for. But to be realistic, one must use genuine dewlap to grind for the dewlap and real poll for the forehead to cover real brain.

Some nights I didn't even come home. But the banquet was worth it, at least from my point of view as an artist. The Black Angus, shrouded with a cloth just like a real sculpture carved in marble, stood in the room's center in a meadow of salad. Surrounding it were the tables for diners, and beyond them, along the room's long sides, were braziers for cooking, sideboards for condiments, tables of bread and rolls of all kinds.

The male guests dressed as cowboys, sheriffs and gamblers, the women as cowgirls. Sarah was dressed as a dancehall queen while I came as a trail cook.

And for the unveiling, I did the honors. As I'd been instructed, I pulled the cord that released the shroud, then backed out of the way. As if the gun for a race had sounded, the diners converged. They cut and tore flesh, the women often with more savagery than their consorts. Then, hands dripping meat juice, they ran to the braziers. Patties were slapped onto the metal of grills, stabbed with spatulas, flipped, slapped again. Steaming meat—often still half raw—was lifted onto slabs of bread and slathered with relish. And so it was eaten.

In twenty minutes, the statue was no more. A memory in blood-pink fragments of ice crystals.

I needed air.

I walked the corridor outside the banquet hall, strolling between steel-lined shelves to the pantry. I turned the corner. And there I saw Sarah.

My princess, my dancehall queen, lay with her skirt hiked above her thighs. And riding on top like a bronco-busting rodeo cowboy, was Peter Collins.

* * *

I wondered later if I should confront her. They hadn't seen me. When we'd gotten home I watched her undress, feeling detached. I thought about art, my wife's body as perfect as one of those Roman statues of Venus.

I thought about beauty, as cold and untouchable—at least for me now—as some of the sculptures I created. Fashioned with love, but for others' enjoyment.

But isn't that always the fate of artists?

* * *

Sarah and I had drawn apart, and we stayed apart this time, even when summer came. When, with its picnics, we usually had fun.

I thought about the fixation she had with men in uniforms. It wasn't her fault; her uncle had been in the Navy. But I wanted, more than I knew, to forgive her.

"Sarah," I said, "I'm going to join the Knights of Columbus. I'm going to show Tony Lagaducci how to make the ship for the banquet so I'll be able to march in the parade."

She didn't answer.

She took to staying out late in the evenings, while I came home early. I wanted to love her. But she didn't know me—she no longer knew me. She didn't understand any more than an artwork I might create understood art.

* * *

Art: *That which is raised to more than ordinary importance;
that which, even if temporary, is forever after etched
in the collective being of man.*

Boars' heads reduced to meat pies for the poor still remain in memory, both for the banqueters on Christmas Eve who see its beauty and those who devour it the following morning. Even the bull at the Cattlemen's Banquet, in its twenty minutes, would not be forgotten.

Thus, art is permanent. And unexpected—a bull torn to pieces?

And Sarah is beauty.

The idea came to me in September with, as is often the case, a commission. The city had recently reinstated its annual Police Awards Banquet—the one that, so long ago, I'd made revolvers for. And I was told, because he had saved a girl from drowning, this year's guest of honor was to be Patrolman Second Class Peter Collins.

I started my drawings. This was to be more than little revolvers. Rather a statue, like the Black Angus, to be unveiled with a shroud and all. My work's culmination.

The theme of the statue: *The Rescued Princess*.

Sarah and I still lived together, however coldly. I never had told her I'd seen her that night, and if she stayed out late more and more evenings, I just smiled and nodded.

"Sarah," I would say, "now that fall's coming and banquet work is starting again, I may have to work late more often myself."

Sometimes she'd answer, "That's okay, Vinnie." She almost always said 'Vinnie' these days.

And then I asked her, "Could you model for me? It's for a commission I want to be special. It's for the policemen."

She smiled when I said that. About policemen. "I guess so, Vinnie. If it won't take too long."

I had her undress, and I drew her beauty into my sketches. I had her pose only for a brief period, in the back pantry, but as the days went by I had her pose more and more often.

"This," I told her, "will be my masterpiece. A statue of you. It's for the centerpiece of the banquet where they're going to give a medal to that policeman, Officer Collins."

I watched her eyes light up when I said 'Collins.'

"That's it," I told her. "That's the expression." I wanted her happy. In the meantime, in the supermarket freezer, I started to build an armature out of plain ice.

Ice? Yes. It *was* unusual, but this sculpture would be dynamic. I molded it after a human skeleton, hollow inside, to hold the meat that would form the body.

I ordered veal—the finest I could get. Using Lagaducci's order forms as always, with his permission, so I could trade back whatever portion might not be needed. This would form the surface. The skin.

And then, just days before the banquet, I got a letter from an uncle in Kansas City. It said he was ill—he was always ill—but this time I wrote back and said I would visit.

"Sarah," I said after supper that night. "I'm going to have to go out of town." I showed her the letter. "I'll finish the statue beforehand, of course, but I'm going to need you to stand in for me on the night of the banquet. Would you mind doing that?"

"You mean..." She was hard pressed to keep the excitement out of her voice. "You mean you want me to go *alone*?"

I nodded. "Yes. And I'm also going to need you to pose for me some more, not just tonight, but tomorrow and the next night as well."

"Oh, Vinnie," she said. "That means I'll have to stay at home every night between now and the banquet. Still..." She gave an elaborate shrug. "If it's for your art, Vinnie...."

"Then you'll do it?"

This time *she* nodded. "But let me freshen up a little before tonight's posing. Okay?"

I kissed her cheek, then went to the pantry to get my things ready. Ten minutes later, I heard her still talking on the hall phone, explaining to whoever it was on the other end that she wouldn't be going out at all for the next few days.

I didn't hurry her.

When at last she came into the pantry, I had the big bend-over freezer open. "Sarah," I said, "why don't you stand there, by Marcino's old grinder? To let the light from the freezer lid reflect on your skin?"

"Okay," she said. I saw she had already unbuttoned her clothing, so I helped her slide it the rest of the way off.

"Now," I said, "let's have you look in the freezer. No, not like you were going to fall in. Tilt your head sideways."

She tried to follow my instructions. I knew she *hated* that aspect of posing.

"That's it," I said. "A little bit more. Close your eyes...just so...."

"Hurry, Vinnie," she said. "It's cold."

"That's right," I said.

I picked up the cleaver.

Struck.

Let the blood run into the freezer. I'd clean it out later.

I started the grinder.

* * *

The next night, straight through to the following day, I worked both at home and at the Eighth Street Supermarket. I finished the sculpture just in time.

My masterpiece.

I bought plane tickets.

* * *

I understand the banquet was to be on local TV. I was in Kansas City, of course, but I'll look up the recording when I'm back in town. I'll have to return when the police call me at my uncle's to tell me that my wife is missing.

I'll play the part of a grieving husband, although I'm sure I'll be suspected. I'll admit that things had gone bad in our marriage. I'll call Sarah's mother to see if she went there. And finally, when there's nothing more that I can do, I'll sell the house and move back to Missouri to start a new life.

The police, to be sure, will have their own ideas—especially after the statue's unveiling by the mayor and what happened under the TV lights afterward. How, with Sarah notably absent from the proceedings, her likeness in meat gleamed under the cameras.

How, when the heat from the lights penetrated the flesh, the hollow ice armature underneath started melting.

How the statue's limbs began to sag, how the breasts started to droop. As if the subject were aging and dying.

How, in an instant, the face caved in.

You see, I had tested it all with models. I knew the moment the legs would crumble. I knew the direction the sculpture would fall, first to its side, then onto its back, the arms swinging forward across the chest.

How, in the simulation of death, my wife would become art. She would be *immortal*.

* * *

Yes, the police will have their ideas. By now they'll already have tested the meat. Wouldn't you send it to the police lab to be analyzed if you were in their place?

What they'll find, when the results come back the following week, is that it is pure veal.

They'll go through my house before they call me. Find everything clean.

Because well before then, Sarah—my princess—will have achieved all that art can accomplish. Her glory not only that night on TV, but even more so, her memory will live through the purchasers of the cellophane-wrapped, oh-so-tender, ground veal patties Lagaducci will have put out on sale the next morning.

ABOUT THE AUTHOR
JAMES S. DORR

James S. Dorr is a short story writer and poet who has published more than four hundred pieces of fiction in a variety of genres. Dorr's latest collection, *The Tears of Isis*, was released by Perpetual Motion Machine Publishing.

Tears of Isis joins his two prose collections from Dark Regions Press, *Strange Mistresses: Tales of Wonder and Romance* and *Darker Loves: Tales of Mystery and Regret*, and the all-poetry *Vamps (A Retrospective)* from Sam's Dot/White Cat Publishing.

An active member of the SFWA and HWA, Dorr's work has also appeared in *Alfred Hitchcock's Mystery Magazine* and *Xenophilia*.

A LETTER TO MY EX
J. MICHAEL MAJOR

Subject: Our daughter, Sydney
Date: 4/28/13 9:58:20 P.M. Central Daylight Time
From: alan_stanton@gmail.com
To: beatrice_ miller_stanton@yoy.com

Beatrice,

By the time you read this, I'll be dead.

Now I'm guessing, depending on the type of day you had, that you either just let out a long, disgusted sigh or spat out a few choice expletives. No doubt you're simply not in the mood for games or another one of my *pathetic* attempts to waste your precious time. It's late, and I know all you want to do is have a glass of wine, maybe take a sleeping pill or two, check your personal e-mail and go to bed. But admit it, your cold heart skipped a hopeful beat, didn't it? Wondering if it's really true?

Oh, I assure you, it is. The poison is already in my system. A canvas bag filled with money lies untouched at the foot of my bed. I'm sure it will disappear with some member of the hotel staff when my body is discovered, but that's not my concern. Right now I need to focus. I have about forty minutes left to write and send this before the poison takes effect.

Was that a whoop of joy? Did you lift your wineglass in a celebratory toast and down its contents in a single gulp? The joyful realization that I'm finally gone for good is likely more than you can handle. Admittedly, you might feel a little sadness at not having me around any longer to publicly and privately berate and humiliate for your own enjoyment, someone to vent your frustrations on, especially since the divorce, but overall, you're probably relieved. No more legal battles, no more visitation rights. Sydney is yours free and clear, no more hassles from me. Your greatest dream comes true.

But, wait a minute. Aren't we supposed to be on a Paris vacation? Didn't Sydney send to your phone those photos of the Eiffel Tower and flowers blooming along the Champs-Elysees? We know you got them because you texted back, hours later, things like "PRETTY" and "NICE" and "HOPE YOU'RE HAVING FUN." All your typical, non-committal responses that mean you're too busy and don't really want to be bothered.

Yes, we were there earlier in the week while you were in Phoenix (supposedly for a seminar, but in reality having a wild fuckfest with your law partners), before returning home to claim sole custody of Sydney forever.

You were rubbing my nose in the fact that from now on I was only going to see her once a month for one hour under strict supervision. It was the only reason you *allowed* me to take her to Paris in the first place.

So, if we're not in Paris, where are we?

In the old days of real letters with pen and paper, right about now you'd be turning the envelope over to check the postmark. But with e-mail you need to trace the servers, and all kinds of other stuff I don't pretend to understand, to find where this message originated. Something the peon interns at your firm could easily do for the senior partner in the morning. But why wait? I'd rather my revenge start immediately. So I'll tell you...

We're in Thailand.

Or rather, by the time you read this, *she's* in Thailand.

Do I have your attention now?

What do you mean, how could I? It's your fault, really. If you hadn't been such a cold, hard, manipulative, lying, cheating, miserable bitch it never would have come to this. But you had to have everything your way, at the expense and happiness and dignity of everyone around you. Including Sydney. And now you're going to pay for it.

Believe me, it wasn't an easy decision. Even now, it tears me apart. While you smothered her with your indifference and took off doing God-knows-what in the name of money and prestige, *I* was the one who always took care of her, especially after being laid-off. I was the one she ran to whenever she was sick or scraped her knee or had a bad dream. I was the one who shared her laughter and helped her with homework. I was the better parent, the one who loved her the most. I know it, you know it, and she knows it.

I have to admit, though, I almost chickened out. When I brought her into the back room of the bar where the sleazy pimp and his armed bodyguards waited for the exchange, I wanted to carry her out of there as fast as I could run away. I couldn't believe that I was going to allow some stranger to harm my beautiful child in ways that I never wanted to think about. But then I remembered what you had done to us and why I was there, and I swallowed my fear and regret and handed her over.

Still, the look of confusion, panic, and terror on her face when that bastard grabbed her arm and yanked her out of the room, and her final, anguished cry of *"Daddy!"* from behind the locked door fills me with the greatest pain I've ever known.

And torturing myself with images of what they might be doing to her *right now* is more agony than I can bear. Though I truly believe it's the right thing to do, it's not something I can live with. That's why I drank the poison as soon as I returned to the hotel room, praying for its imminent relief.

But not before I finish this letter to you.

Maybe they won't use her right away. I suppose it's a possibility. It might, in fact, be smart to hold her for a while. Making her stand naked in front of countless drooling, disgusting perverts and keeping her isolated until the best offer is received. A blonde, blue-eyed, nine-year-old virgin will no doubt fetch a hefty sum in this part of the world, an offer and amount her pimp will capitalize on repeatedly for as long as she remains the sobbing, terror-filled, cowering, rented victim of some sick beast.

How many nights will she spend with her hands pressed between her legs, blood seeping through her fingers, crying and shaking from the pain of her torn labia? Or dry-heaving from the taste of semen in her mouth? But eventually the wear and abuse will become apparent in her mannerisms, and on her body and face, and she'll be dumped in with the other forgotten, sold, stolen, abandoned and unwanted children forced to ply this vile and despicable trade here.

I wonder if she will be housed in squalid, crowded rooms without heat or running water? Just think, she might even catch malaria, hemorrhagic fever, dysentery, cholera, or any number of other diseases that could potentially be a blessing, when you think about it.

Will she find any friends among the other enslaved children, someone to help ease the pain of her horrible new life? Or will she be an outcast, shunned and ignored at best? Maybe she'll even be beaten by her fellow victims because of jealousy due to some supposed preferential treatment, or simply because of her skin color and inability to speak their language. Abused by both the men paying for her body and her fellow captives, her every waking moment will be a living hell.

And what of the times she tries to sleep? Will her dreams be filled with nightmares of the daily pain? Or will she instead find solace in memories of vacations and school events and birthday parties? Like her eighth birthday, when we gave her the go-cart. Watching her riding around and around the driveway and up and down the street, her pigtails flying in the breeze behind her and the biggest smile on her face. I swear, I've never seen her happier. Will memories like this console her throughout the day, providing a sanctuary for her mind to escape to, or will they torment and mock her even more?

Then, you ask, how could I do this, if I truly loved her the most? The truth is it really isn't about her. You're the one who gave me the idea. Though I'd better explain quickly, because my fingers are growing numb.

Frankly, I've always wondered if you had any maternal instincts at all. Guess we'll find out now, won't we? Or, as I truly believe, it was always just a matter of appearances. And control.

Like how you'd parade us around at your office Christmas parties: the beautiful, smart, dutiful child who looked so much like her mother, and the worthless husband who hasn't been able to find a job in the three years since his company downsized. The doting mother and long-suffering wife, who was able to bear the burden of a full-time career while heroically holding her family together. Give me a fucking break!

The fact that I paid all the bills until I lost my position of eighteen years and single-handedly put you through law school somehow managed to be left out of those representations of character. Amazing, isn't it?

You never wanted them to know what you were *really* like, did you? That wouldn't do for your carefully molded image. Like what you did to Sydney's go-cart, remember? When she brought home a report card a few months later with a 'B' on it, and you went *berserk*, smashing the go-cart to pieces with a sledgehammer while Sydney cried and begged for you to stop. But you wouldn't listen. You just reduced it to bits as you yelled and screamed how no daughter of yours was going to be '*weak*,' to be '*stupid*,' to be a '*failure like her father.*' And it angered you even more when she ran to me for comfort afterward. It was more than your twisted, manipulative, control-freak mind could bear. You couldn't handle the fact that she loved me more than she *feared* you.

And so came the divorce.

But what you did at the custody hearing was *beyond* unforgivable. You knew she wanted to live with me, and that was something your ego wouldn't allow. So, using the facts that the courts are already biased against fathers and that I couldn't financially support her on my own right now, you fabricated the whole story about how I had sexually abused her for years, and that it was you who needed sole custody in order to protect her.

Then you sealed the deal by blowing the judge in his chambers. What, you think I didn't know? You miserable cunt! How could you do something like that to us? To *her*?! You know for a fact that the abuse never happened, because neither you nor the courts would *ever* have allowed me to take her to Paris while you went on your fuckfest.

It's all about manipulation, though, isn't it, bitch? And you always get your way.

It was this final insult on an already beaten down man that threw me over the edge. You always thought you were sooooo clever, but you pushed me too far this time. Taking my daughter, the light of my life, away from me and saddling me for the rest of my life with false allegations that were accepted as fact without ever having to be proven in a court of law. Not giving me the chance to defend myself against such insane and preposterous lies was more than I could handle. And so, later that night while I cried in bed, unable to sleep, I decided to bring her here. To Thailand. To teach you a lesson you'll never forget.

Damn, I'm really sweating now. My hands are beginning to tremble and it's getting harder to type. I need to hurry. My clock is ticking.

You're probably wondering why I didn't kill Sydney then, to put her out of her misery. The news is filled with stories of parents murdering their own children to prevent losing custody. Fathers beating or shooting the kids, and mothers poisoning or drowning them in bathtubs or by driving the family car into a lake. Why didn't I just do that?

The truth is I could never personally harm her. Hell, I've never even spanked her, which is more than I can say for you. And frankly, it boiled down to the fact that after all those years of silently tolerating your verbal abuse, I couldn't leave you with an easy sense of closure. No, I *needed* you to suffer too.

Oh, I'll admit that knowing what a hell on earth her life was going to become, I briefly considered hiding her with a relative or friend, or squirreling her away in some state-run facility in some foreign country. After all, she is my daughter, and I love her very much. But I knew that you, with all your resources and connections at the law firm, your controlling tenacity, you would find her somehow, either through guilt or legal intimidation or media blitzkrieg, and the person I'd entrusted with her safety would return Sydney to you as soon as my lifeless body was found. No, I couldn't risk it.

So then, why *did* I do it? Haven't you figured it out yet?

I'm preventing you from turning her into a replica of the most worthless piece of shit I've ever known. I did it to keep her from becoming *you*.

Oh, goddamnit! I just vomited blood on the keyboard. Fuck fuck fuck!

I've got to get this done. I'm becoming disoriented and spending far too much time correcting typos. I need to finish this and send it before the poison completely incapacitates me. Then I can sleep forever.

But will *you* ever be able to sleep again?

It's possible you might simply say, 'Oh well, two less problems to worry about.' But I doubt it. I think those long-buried maternal instincts will take over. If nothing else, the controlling cunt in you simply won't *allow* this to happen. The adrenaline rush will kick in and you'll use every available resource at your disposal.

But over time, you'll become daunted by the sheer magnitude of the almost impossible odds of finding her. What town or village did I leave her in? Will she be hidden away, never allowed outside where others might see her? Or will they move her about, to other countries even?

Your days will be spent frantically searching for her, but your nights will be filled with endless terrors, images of what they might be doing to her *at that very moment.* Nightmares will suck the very life out of the remainder of your pathetic existence.

Sleep deprivation. Obsessive, hopeless searches. Facing impossible odds. I die a happy man knowing what's ahead for you.

My vision's so blurry now I can barely see. I can't stop shaking, and my heart is pounding so hard I'm afraid it will burst. Not that you care, I know. Just got to make sure I hit SEND before I collapse on the floor.

One final note, however, before I leave. They say the best way to hurt someone who has lost everything is to give that person back something that is broken. Even if you somehow find her and come riding in with the cavalry or Black Ops or Navy SEALS, believe me, she *will* be damaged. Because, after her eyes widened when the Thai pimp handed me the canvas bag of money and yanked her away from me, the last thing I told her was that this was *your* idea.

So sleep tight, if you can. But my faith in your imminent breakdown tells me otherwise. Serves you right for what you put us through. I'd say I'll see you in Hell, but I know you're already there.

Fuck you, bitch. I'm outta here.

Alan

[SEND]

ABOUT THE AUTHOR
J. MICHAEL MAJOR

A member of the Horror Writers Association and the Mystery Writers of America, J. Michael Major's first novel, *One Man's Castle*, was recently published by Five Star/Cengage.

Jay Bonansinga, *New York Times* bestselling co-author of *The Walking Dead: Rise of the Governor*, calls Major's novel a "... crazy quilt of crime, horror, and psychological weirdness."

Major has had three dozen short stories published in such anthologies as *DeathGrip 3: It Came From the Cinema* and *New Traditions in Terror*, and magazines that include *Bare Bone*, *Hardboiled*, *Pirate Writings*, *Into the Darkness*, *Outer Darkness* and *The Sterling Web*.

DEVIL RIDES SHOTGUN
ERIC DEL CARLO

Detective Joaquim Abito, twenty-two years after lacing up his polished Florsheims on the morning of Academy graduation, and now teetering on the brink of mental-emotional-spiritual collapse, drove out to the desolate crossroads at midnight and summoned a demon.

It was something you learned on the force, if you worked the bloodiest cases long enough and didn't retreat to a pussy desk post. Some older detective might hip you to the stygian underside of police work.

For Joaquim, it had been Det. Sal Popovich. Sal, whose craggy face had looked like a mountainside after an avalanche, was hard-drinking and hard-driven, using up wives as fast as his liver. He had been a committed cop. Normal people never understood that the real ones did the job full-out. No restraints and no squeamish-ness. Use everything. Risk anything. To hell with consequences.

Sal Popovich's rough face wavered momentarily in Abito's un-steady mind's eye, then erupted into a goulash of blood, bone and matter. He'd eaten the licorice. Joaquim had seen the body be-fore the bag boys came. He hadn't flinched or even looked away. Sal had shot himself in his easy chair, with the game on the TV, and hadn't given a cold fuck about the mess that sprayed his living room. Det. Abito took that as a final lesson from his mentor.

Truth be told, he'd seen himself following Sal someday. Angeli-ca had finally left and taken their daughter, long after both females had become strangers to him. Joaquim understood that doing the job with unchecked fervor meant collateral damage. The trick was never to calculate too carefully the price you or others were paying for this hallowed work.

Killers had to pay. Human vermin needed to be stomped out.

Det. Joaquim Abito vowed he would get The Sculptor before his own string played out and he too tasted the barrel. Toward that end, he had decided to conjure this demon from the depths of Hell.

Roads crossed everywhere in this country, on this world. Abito, caught in the fever of his gruesome, giddy endeavor, had chosen tonight's junction with a keen eye. It lay outside the economically depressed, crime-riddled city of his jurisdiction. One was a weedy, rutted track that belonged to the early years of the previous centu-ry; used by a farmer named Colvin, who had sired and slaughtered four daughters, killing each girl in her infancy with impunity in what were then isolated hinterlands. The wife, lurid diary entries eventually revealed, allowed the murders, as she shared her husband's strong desire for a son. That faded but still visible cart path was crossed by a gravely back road that led through scrub tracts to a swamp. Sociopathic male teenagers at three district high schools proudly referred to the unlit lane as Rape Row.

Abito had navigated his precious 1971 GTO down this road to the crossing. Cherry condition, cobalt blue finish, hardtop. The 400 V8 growled throatily even as he inched it along, headlights doused. The auto was his one indulgence, the single luxury he'd allowed in a life otherwise maniacally devoted to the job.

Now the car sat on the shoulder, and the aging detective stood outside a circle of guttering candles. Virginal blood, courtesy of the city morgue and a nine-year-old boy who'd unwisely tried to stop his father from once again bashing his mother's face to mush, coated Joaquim's left hand. In his right he held the musty book that Sal Popovich had recommended. The ancient words tangled his tongue and made his eyeballs throb. He sweated beneath his shabby suit.

Overhead, the stark stars wheeled. The night lay bleak. He had been at this some interminable time, reciting passages, splashing the circle with blood, scattering the scene with the prescribed animal bones. The smoking tallow candles threw lunatic shadows onto his stubbly, damp features. Again and again he offered up his soul, which was of course the cost of this venture.

That small part of Det. Abito's mind still operating with something near to rationality put forward a suggestion: *This is crazy; maybe I should stop.*

At that instant, however, the nighttime...split.

Joaquim thought of throats slashed ear-to-ear streaming

blood, of maggot-crawling wounds opened like mouths on putre-
fied corpses, of cunts—all the elliptical rents in human flesh he had
seen and been horrified by in his time.

This one opened on the crossroads, and out of it seeped queasy
curls of gangrenous fog and howls of agony beyond mortal madness. Deep black roiled far inside the rent, midnight flames licking
a toxic landscape. Impossibly abhorrent creatures—jackals with
leprous bat wings, cockroaches the size of dinosaurs with the faces
of retarded children—swarmed at each other, gnashing and eating
voraciously.

A biting wind and the reek of what just had to be brimstone
staggered Abito back several steps. The arcane volume flew out of
his hand, brittle pages flapping. The candles extinguished as they
tumbled away, the animal bones clattering after.

Despite the inconceivable depths revealed by the gash, the ap-
erture itself was of modest size. Out of it now emerged a human-
sized shape of vaguely human-like dimensions. Legs, torso, arms,
tail—

Yes, tail. Whipping behind with authority. The stride was confident, the bearing almost regal. The demon was fantastically ugly,
like a great, suppurating wound, like road kill cooked on asphalt
for a week. Like deceit, jealousy, malice—all these things animated
and made flesh.

Yet, the infernal being was equipped with enough human char-
acteristics to be described as *he*. And as he approached Det. Abito,
grinning, he was the one who said, "Okay, let's get to work," and
crossed toward the GTO, tail switching eagerly.

The ellipse-shaped breach snapped shut, and the agonized
screams died in the empty midnight.

Joaquim had to hurry to his car to get there before the demon.

* * *

Don't let the hellish fucker distract you.

So Sal had instructed him, when Joaquim grew desperate and deranged enough to believe the older detective's stories about demonic summonings.

It'll want to deceive you. Keep it on message. You conjured it, you control it.

"We call him The Sculptor," Abito said, knuckles white on the steering wheel, even those of his blood-tacky hand. They were heading back toward the city. "Newspapers and bloggers were calling him Rodin for a while, but the public didn't get the reference so—" He cut himself off. Unnecessary information. He too needed to stay focused. His heart pounded furiously, with excitement, with fear. Maybe with disbelief too. After all, he had a bona fide demon in his passenger seat.

"Rodin. *The Thinker*, right?" That demon spoke with a human cadence, even if the voice was pitched far too low for normal vocal chords. Still, his intonations were confident, like a foreigner who had learned perfect English.

"Right," Abito said. "Now, The Sculptor—"

"This is a '71. A Pontiac. The real thing, not a reproduction." The creature was looking all about the car's interior.

Joaquim had great affection for the automobile. Really, it occupied the lone warm space in his heart that might have been reserved for a wife and daughter in another man. "Authentic GTO," he said proudly. Then he kicked himself mentally.

Don't let him distract.

"It's cherry," said the demon, grinning again with a mouthful of what most resembled shark's teeth. His features were chaotic, revolting, yet cast in a masculine mold. His appreciation for the car, too, had a manly quality about it.

But his body was like a black, glistening shell, pumping with ulcers. His feet were talons, his hands claws, and his eye sockets swirled with sulphurous smoke.

Det. Abito started to shake, a profound shuddering that came up from his marrows. It got hold of the joints of his limbs, help-lessly jerking knees and hips, shoulders and wrists. He stomped the car's brakes and showered the narrow, dim way ahead with gravel.

He couldn't remember the last time he'd slept or eaten—or, actually, he could remember, but not a night of restorative sleep, nor a meal which hadn't tasted like sawdust and settled like lead. Even the ordinary pleasures had been stripped out of his life. This latest bloody case—the worst yet—had consumed him.

The interior of the car felt frighteningly close all of a sudden. The hardtop pressed on his skull, the hand-rolled windows squeezed against his flanks. He was going to be crushed together with this vile entity in the passenger seat. Had this undertaking already failed? Had he let control slip away?

Something touched his trembling arm, but he didn't flinch away from it, not even when he saw it was the demon's long-nailed, grimy hand. The touch was quite light, and it didn't burn or freeze or do any of what you might expect a demon's touch to do.

"Hey," the impossibly bass voice said with a just as impossible gentleness. "I only came because of the car. No one from this world can just invoke us, you know. We choose, and if we do, then we commit. I want to ride in your car. The Pontiac GTO is the pinnacle of American automobile manufacture. Whatever else happens tonight happens. I smell cop on you, so you want to catch someone. Now"—the demon shifted on the seat and his tail switched between his legs—"tell me all about...The Sculptor."

* * *

The room was hot with blood. Literally. Abito felt the released human heat on his own skin, coating him, sucking away oxygen the way a brutally humid high summer day always seemed to, so that you were taking air in tiny sips and your head felt light.

He had come to the scene with assumptions, with a sense of preparedness which he had earned after years of doing this particular horrific work. Most people walked through life and faced their petty horrors, suffered their commonplace tragedies, wept in bad times and got out of the game at the end without ever truly witnessing the ghastliness human beings were capable of inflicting upon others of their same species.

Joaquim Abito had more than observed such things. He had, in the course of his grim duties, been made to wallow in the atrocities. He had visited crime scenes, seen the aftermaths and reconstructed the circumstances of veritable abominations, acts of depravity and cruelty beyond any pale you would care to name. These things had changed him, to be sure. It was why Det. Popovich's suicide, when it came several weeks later, would not really affect him, beyond him thinking, *Sal probably had the right idea.*

But when Det. Abito entered the blood-warmed room and saw

what awaited him, he beheld a proof, concluding and irrefutable, of the degeneracy, the iniquity, the heartlessness of the human animal.

A uniformed officer stood present, green-faced, swaying, looking at Abito with maddened, pleading eyes. She had been left to guard the scene until the detective's arrival.

"Get out of here," Joaquim told her in a whisper, and she bolted gracelessly out of the room, out of the apartment building, which was a moldering Victorian long since divided into separate living units. This was the second story apartment.

Abito breathed the hot, still, coppery air.

The *thing* occupied the center of the one big room, to which a sink, cupboards and refrigerator were attached along one wall. The apartment's bedroom was closet-sized; maybe it had been a closet once, in the house's past. Still, it wasn't a squalid dwelling. It felt like a woman lived here, though the detective saw no definitive telltales as to the occupant's gender.

He had no doubt, however, that the *thing* standing atop a carefully arranged tarp of spread newspapers on a hardwood floor would turn out to be the apartment's tenant. But there was no telling the sex, the ethnicity or even the original dimensions of the person. Perhaps one third—cold anatomical analyses would later reveal it to be almost precisely that amount—of the mass had been removed.

Inside the block of marble the statue already exists.

The human body was not a solid article, by any means. It could be said to be a gelatinous sack. But there was enough material to work with, even after the vast bleeding that came of removing that containing outer layer. Abito had taken two steps toward the

thing, and the toe of his scuffed, brown shoe—his natty graduation Florsheims were long buried in a closet—pressed the edge of
one of the saturated newspaper sheets. Bubbles squelched from
beneath the soaked paper.

Joaquim withdrew his foot, took a slow, half step back.

Bone was, of course, solid. Sinew and muscle had tensile sub-
stance, and certain of the firmer internal organs could be coaxed
and molded. There was enough *there* there. After that, it fell to the
skill of the shaper's hands and the sharpness of his instruments.

The talent was evident. What had been surgically removed lay
on the floor, all about the finished piece, blobs and globs like dis-
carded clay. What remained was a careful, concise structure, with
obvious artistic purpose. To think of it as a *thing* was, Joaquim
Abito knew, unfair.

He circled it now, and his steps fell nearly soundlessly in the
torrid, reeking room, whose windows were beaded with condensation. He got a full appreciative look at the work, because it was his
job to look, no matter the extreme of the horror.

It was a girl, a child. Her head hung slightly in angelic repose,
and hands lay folded on her boyish chest. Her features were explic-
itly defined—tiny nose, shy jawline, a mouth made demure. She
stood at a bashful angle. Were this chiseled in milk-white marble,
the image would be heartbreaking, lovely, truthful. Instead, the
child had been rendered in the medium of adult human meat.

The detective felt neurons misfiring in his brain. Segment by
segment his bowels tightened. It was a growing certainty that he
was going to vomit in a nearby sink. But even these intense but
predictable physiological reactions didn't hide the fact that what
he saw here was something new to him. This was *obscenity*, and

he had not encountered its like in twenty-two years of police work.

He would, he vowed then, do anything to bring justice to this ultimate transgression, this vilest, most unimaginable of crimes. Anything. Any...thing.

* * *

"So, you're a crusader, huh? The hand of justice?" The shark's teeth gleamed in that pustulant face.

"I know I have to get this guy."

"Duty? Moral obligation? It's hard understanding you humans a lot of the time. You tie yourself up in such knots."

Abito ignored the mockery, if that was what it was. He didn't figure he could impress his own morality on this being from the Pit. "What we know about The Sculptor is that he does his work where and when he wants. Five of these...incidents. No one ever sees him come or go. He leaves nothing for forensics."

"What do you think of his work?" The demon draped an arm over the back of his seat.

Don't let him distract you.

"Artistically, I mean. You must have an opinion. You've seen all his pieces, after all."

The trembling tried to start up again, working outward from Joaquim's bone marrow, but he held it off by furious force of will. "I am taking you to the last crime scene." He gritted out the words one by one. "That's what you need, right? To get a scent on him or whatever?" Sal had told him how it worked.

They were off the gravel lane by now, onto a frontage road.

The city lights shone ahead. Abito had the headlights on, and had cleaned the virgin's blood from his hand with a wet wipe. The GTO's V8 growled with new authority as he opened it up some. His heart continued to hammer, but the urgency of tonight's deed drove it now.

The demon let out a guttural sigh, luxuriating in the leather passenger seat. "Yep, this is one sweet ride."

* * *

The home was single-storied, a strip of yard front and back, garage attached. Generic. In fact, it looked infuriatingly like every other dwelling on the block. Abito didn't object to the aesthetics. Certainly this was a more respectable place than where he lived. But the house's anonymity with regard to its neighbors begged that maddening police question: *Why here, and not someplace else?* Which was intimately related to the worst question of all: *Why this victim, and not some other?*

The city block lay still, unmoving. Not a porch light lit, not a curtain drawn back from any window that the detective could see in either direction as he stepped out of the Pontiac at the curb. Surely someone was awake, he thought. Surely sleepless nights were now the norm for these nearby residents on Rosario Way. What had happened here, at number 392, had to have struck a primordial fear into their hearts.

Abito had given the demon a faded black duster to wear. Hopefully the creature's humanoid shape would help with the disguise. But even if somebody watching their arrival through window blinds and fear-narrowed eyes were to perceive the demon, Joaquim didn't much care. He was fully committed to this. The consequences meant almost nothing.

He crossed to 392's front door. Behind, the loaner coat swished as the demon followed. Talons scraped the concrete. It was the sound of stick matches against their striker strip, a sound from his childhood—his mother lighting burners on the solid, dingy stove in the kitchen, making oatmeal for him and his sister on fog-bound autumn mornings.

A small, rubbery and completely out-of-control smile passed across his lips before he pressed it dead. He held his breath for a beat of three, standing at the door. Then he swiftly rifled the lock and entered with the demon still in tow.

He flicked on a pocket flashlight for his own benefit. Doubtless this demon's sulphurously smoking eyes could see in the dark, accustomed as they must be to darknesses malevolent, repellent and beyond mortal scope.

"Here is where it was." Abito played the light's narrow strong beam on the empty space at the center of the living room. He didn't need to make any effort to recollect the scene. It was like he'd never left it.

The demon glided past him, and in the funhouse-spooky flashlight-lit interior of the empty home the Hellish creature appeared even more monstrous, a thing you saw from the corner of your eye at two AM when you had a bad fever. The sight curdled Joaquim, but didn't weaken his resolve.

Taloned feet scratched back and forth over the floor a moment. Then the being stopped and cocked his head. "Tell me what you saw."

Abito had prepared himself for this inevitability. He recounted the scene, omitting nothing. He described what The Sculptor had left behind on this, his fifth ghastly effort. It was possible the demon was just playing with him, forcing him to relive the terrible episode. But the images of that day, along with those of the four other crime scenes, were permanently fused into his thoughts and memories.

Here, for the first time, The Sculptor had worked with multiple subjects. Abito knew the names of the father and his two children—a girl of seventeen and a boy of fourteen, burly for his age. He knew the daughter had a boyfriend and ambitions to breed show ponies. The son fit on his school team's offensive line like he'd been born there. The father was content, proud, plodding.

The Sculptor had made monkeys out of them.

It was another first for the nameless, freakish man. There wasn't even evidence enough to say this was a man, but absolutely everyone thought the perpetrator male—a heretofore unseen hint of drollery. The work sustained the dizzyingly high level of craftsmanship. No one had ever worked in such a manner with these particular materials, and nobody could ever achieve such rarefied artistic heights again. But up until this venture the works had been somber, achingly lovely—which, naturally, made them all the more grotesque.

Now, however, The Sculptor had apparently turned toward slapstick. But the skill was still there. The three monkeys, all of a size, were conscientiously rendered. The details were exquisite—bristling fur, wide nostrils, hunched postures. Small, artful, simian hands covered eyes, ears and mouth, respectively. The sculpted figures stood in a neat row.

See no evil, hear no evil, speak no—

The demon stood silent a long moment after Det. Abito had finished. He waited. Finally the creature said in his bass voice, "This is a talent at work."

"Yes," Abito agreed. No way to deny that.

Another silence swelled in the dim living room where the detective had stood days before, his brain caving in on itself, his nerves buzzing and popping like faulty electrical connections. He had seen the end coming for him then, black and unhurried, the dull sting of metal on his tongue as he inserted the barrel, the appalling final seconds when he would want to change his mind. The act itself wasn't so bad. But he revolted utterly against the possibility of leaving these crimes unanswered.

"There's something else, though..."

Joaquim Abito snapped the flashlight's tight, white cone toward the shape in the black duster. Scabrous shell-flesh glimmered between the coat's folds. "What is it?" the detective asked sharply.

Smoke spun where eyes should be. Yet the expression had a special intensity. The demon said, "He's not doing this alone."

"No?" Joaquim's voice was suddenly faint.

"He's got help. Help from my neck of the woods. Your guy's working with another demon." The shark teeth, framed by foul lips, this time showed in a grimace.

* * *

"We've got rules," the demon said, his ghastly face worsened by the dashboard glow lighting him from underneath.

"Rules?" asked Abito dubiously.

"Codes then. What, you think you sad little creatures *own* the concept?"

The detective concentrated on steering the Pontiac through the city streets. The demon was angry, or at least annoyed, and Joaquim didn't want to draw any of that toward him. Still, he remained curious about this turn of events.

After a minute, Abito driving in the direction he'd been told to, the demon gave a gruff sigh. "There are just things...you don't do. Among my kind. We're not top dogs, you know. Not in our hierarchy. We're middle types, a full tier down from the big boys, the ones who matter, who make the decisions. But we have our own... standards." He shook his head forcefully, and a few drops of what looked like sputum hit the windshield. "We don't interfere like this!"

Abito, bewildered, hesitated to speak. They were on Califax Street, cruising north. Permanently dim warehouses with crumbling loading docks walled the way. Lots of businesses had pulled out of here.

Finally, though, curiosity got the best of him. "Interfere how?" he murmured, half hoping his passenger wouldn't hear the question.

But the demon did. "You think these crimes are utterly horrifying, right? The work of The Sculptor—an unimaginable evil. Hah! It's a gag, a lark, a cheap juvenile stunt. My kind works in torment. It is our medium. We take the souls of the damned and show them what *damned* means."

Abito swallowed a cold, greasy something in his throat. He knew the deal here. Sal Popovich had explained that too. You could summon a demon, you could have him do your bidding, but you would pay in the end. The price was one human soul. And Joaquim had put up his, all to see The Sculptor brought to justice.

"Your human who likes to make the meat carvings? He must have tried to conjure a demon. What astounds me is that one answered. We don't go in for this amateurish nonsense. It's beneath us. It's...contemptible."

The demon shook his head again, slower this time, with what seemed to Abito like genuine chagrin.

They were coming up on the end of Califax Street, where it dead-ended into littered lots surrounded by chain-link. The detective asked, "Do I turn here?" The last cross street was approaching.

"Pull up there." The demon gestured with a curt indifference at the nearby curb. Abito wondered—the thought pulling at him like an undertow—if all this was just the runaround. Maybe this Hellish denizen had never meant to help him.

The cobalt-colored GTO gave a last snarl as he cut the ignition.

An elevated freeway stood a block away, its supports massive and painted with shadows and graffiti. The traffic upon it provided a steady thrumming sound that reminded Abito of circulating blood heard through a stethoscope. He and the demon stepped out of the car, the other still wearing the faded black duster. A final warehouse occupied the street; a grim, sturdy, seedy place with ranks of dark, reinforced windows and ocher brickwork that would take another century to turn to powder.

"He's in there?" the detective asked, his whisper high-pitched and childlike to his ears. He felt inside his rumpled suit for the holster, the familiar weight of his gun.

The shark-like teeth shone in the struggling orange light of the nearest streetlamp. "Your guy and mine," he said. A large rusted sliding door stood a few feet away. He took a talon-scratching step toward it, then paused, looking back. "What's your name anyway?"

"Abito. Joaquim Abito. You?"

"Call me Gu'ueyun."

The detective grunted a laugh. "I'll try." It was like one of the tongue-tangling words he'd recited earlier from the musty tome, part of the incantations that had started all this.

They moved on the door.

The lock was unyielding, industrial. Abito had tools and experience and probably could have gotten past the door in time, but Gu'ueyun was impatient now. He put his claw to the flaky metal and pungent smoke rose, followed by a soft clank. Abito seized the handle and drew carefully, and the wide rectangle moved on nearly silent, oiled tracks. The corroded door should have squealed like a maimed animal; it hadn't. This *abandoned* building was in use.

Gu'ueyun went in first this time, Joaquim following close enough to feel the brushing tail of the duster. He had his pistol in hand, thumb to the hammer, mildly arthritic index finger on the trigger. Beyond the door a truly cavernous space opened up. He sensed the echoing emptiness, the soaring ceiling, the damp odor of disuse. But beneath that soddenness another scent inhabited the unlit expanse, a fresher smell, something...active.

It was far too large an area for condensation on the windows, or for the release of internal body heat to be felt at a distance. But you couldn't hide that scent. It was almost a taste.

Abito strained to see. For a dizzied second or two he wished he too had eyes of swirling sulphur smoke that could penetrate the dimness. Right now he wanted every edge, every advantage. He didn't care if any of this was a cheat. If anything like that had still counted, he wouldn't have set out this midnight to enlist a demon to his cause. Tonight he would have The Sculptor. Nothing—literally, *nothing*—else mattered.

The warehouse's interior seemed to expand beyond its limits, a great shadowy grotto which went on and on past its own walls, like the glimpse of infinite roiling darkness the detective had gotten earlier through the elliptical rent. This place, though, wasn't Hell. It was earth-bound and tangible.

He started to see. Shapes grew out of the shadows. This place had been emptied, but some of the fixtures remained. There was piping overhead, the shell of an office against one wall. Something rattled, and Abito's eyes, pupils expanded in a weary, weathered face, caught movement.

Something dangled from a section of crisscrossing pipe.

The demon went flashing away from him, moving with only the faintest rasp of talon on concrete. Joaquim halted briefly, taking in what he saw, exercising a last, pale policeman's instinct of caution, of judicious appraisal before making a decisive move.

The soft, wan, incredibly vulnerable body, hung by a length of chain from a pipe above, was causing the links to rattle gently. But it didn't merely sway. There was still movement in that form, a weak, jerky, desperate animation that should have been impossible.

You didn't even *want* the person to still be alive at this point.

Once, Abito had arrived at a car wreck moments after it occurred, beating the paramedics and everybody else to the scene. The auto had caromed off a light stanchion before pounding into the stone steps of a library. The driver was halfway through his windshield, and as Abito approached, he was methodically and determinedly tearing his way free of the glass. Three quarters of his scalp was flopped over one side of his face and most of his fingers were attached to his hands by glistening threads. His shirt was shredded, and his chest had been flayed. The complex movement of every muscle was visible, the sublime design laid bare like a living anatomical diagram. The man left hunks of himself in the frosted, shattered sheet of the windshield glass. He stepped free of his demolished car and looked directly at Abito who stood frozen several feet away. The driver carefully swept the dripping swath of his scalp back up onto his skull with a mutilated hand, and finally fell over with a heavy wet smack. Abito remembered thinking, *Thank God.*

This was worse. It was worse because it was deliberate and observant. The patient concentration of a research scientist had gone into this endeavor.

A harness held the naked body, something sturdy and buckled that caught under the arms. And her nakedness—it was indeed a woman—went beyond mere exposure of skin; there was nothing to titillate even the most desperately virginal adolescent. A paring had begun here in this isolated warehouse. It was far from complete, but already a sizable sheet of outer covering had been removed from the torso.

But here was the new thing The Sculptor had learned to do. With his previous effort at 392 Rosario Way, he had worked for the first time with a plurality of subjects instead of the usual single. But with that case and the others before it, the victims had all been well and truly dead. Ploddingly efficient police work had at least verified that much.

This time, he was keeping his subject alive.

Of course, Joaquim Abito knew, he had help. He'd had it all along. Coming and going at the crime scenes at will, taking his time to work with the meat and bone, making his artful shapes, seemingly without worry of interruption. It was The Sculptor's confederate that had made that possible.

Abito thought of Rosario Way and the neighbors who didn't look out their windows when they'd entered number 392. That had to be the influence of Gu'ueyun. Of the creature's powers, he had only known that the demon could find The Sculptor for him. So long as Abito agreed to pay the cost. Abito had so pledged.

And now here was The Sculptor. The dirty fucker about his vile work.

The detective moved toward him now, at a run. The Sculptor was indeed male, as everybody had guessed; or maybe it was that no one could fit these abominable acts anywhere within the purview of the feminine character, which might have been prejudicial, or might have been flattering. The glimpses Abito had as he raced across the floor of the warehouse showed him a man of mundane detail—not ugly, not fat, not tall, not even engagingly ordinary-looking in the way of movie character actors. This was the guy on the bus in the second to last seat from the back, the man ahead of you in line ordering the small house coffee to go. Scenery dressing, inoffensive and inconsequential.

Joaquim charged down on him, pistol at the ready, as The Sculptor—what a plain name he would surely turn out to have, such as Brent Johns or Stew Baker—drew a fresh seam across the woman's flesh with some small, hooked instrument. He wore a rain poncho, one of the cheap ones that was little more than a garbage bag with holes for your arms. A small lamp lit his work-space.

The plump, pale, thoroughly bloodied woman quivered, and again the chain rattled. Her face was lacquered with sweat, and she had already passed the point where she could produce speech or even sound. There was no telling at this stage what shape was being produced here, what the final form would be. Surely, though, this woman couldn't stay alive much longer, no matter what infernal influence was at work here. *Lucky for her.*

The man turned from his work, nondescript face pinched with annoyance, as Abito centered the revolver on The Sculptor's chest. There would be no arrest, no trial, no allowance for the slow grinding of judicial wheels. Det. Abito had seen and judged, and now it was time to close this case.

A feral cry suddenly blared through the warehouse, ear-piercing, a lunatic screech, loud enough to cause the fillings in Joaquim's teeth to stab his jaw painfully. At nearly the same instant, two grappling bodies spun and tumbled into view, just at the sepia-toned edge of the work lamp's circle of light. Limbs tipped with wicked sharpness flailed madly. One of the creatures tore something flapping and dark off the back of the other. Abito thought it was flesh, but a heartbeat later saw it was only a part of the black duster. The two demons rolled back toward the dimmer reaches of the warehouse, and another hideously shrill shriek reverberated.

Abito, who had skidded to a halt, snapped his eyes back toward The Sculptor where he stood by the chained, dangling woman. The ordinary-looking man had raised his hand-sized hooked implement high up above his right shoulder and was about to bring it down in a swooping slash. The detective's finger jerked, not a smooth pull like they taught you at the Academy, but the gun discharged anyway. A quarter-shaped dot appeared on The Sculptor's chest, satisfyingly centered, and the force of the slug at close range took him right off his feet. He hit the cement ground with a fleshy thud.

Joaquim followed. Two steps forward, lift the pistol again, two more shots, one into the forehead, the other his face—that last just a desecration, a well-deserved one.

The muzzle flashes left him blinking, and the smell of burnt gunpowder dizzied him. But when he turned and looked up, he still caught the faint flicker crossing the woman's mouth, a tiny twist of lips that indicated a positive emotion. Maybe satisfaction. Maybe gratitude. After that, though, her face quieted and her eyes closed. He wanted to believe it was slow serenity. One link clinked softly against another, but the woman was now only swaying.

The animal-frenzy screaming went on, and the combatants came into view several more times. Abito could do nothing. He stood over his own victim and watched, strangely detached. The proceedings were violent, blood-curdling, and the next time one of the demons tore away something from the other, it was a claw full of festering flesh. The detective didn't know who had wounded who, if the wound was decisive, or which of the two was winning. He couldn't even guess how a victory would be determined. After all, could one denizen of Hell kill another? And what would the death of a demon mean?

But the final attack did indeed look final to Abito. One dribbling, staggering demon tried now to retreat from the other, holding mangled parts of itself together. The other pounced. Arms worked at blurring speed, long-nailed fingers at full extension. The head snapped forward, and rows of teeth did their work. It went on for some time, until cankerous meat lay everywhere, some barely connected to bone or sinew, the rest scattered into dark, nameless chunks. The screeching had stopped a while ago.

Gu'ueyun stood, stretched carefully and came to Abito. He paused to glance up at the dead, chained woman. The work lamp was still on, and the detective imagined he read scorn in the smoke-swirling eye sockets. The demon muttered, "Amateur hour." There was no mistaking his disgusted tone.

* * *

The GTO handled, as always, perfectly. This time going down the gravelly lane Abito had the headlights on. Ahead, the road rocked gently. Starlight fell on the semi-rural scenery. At the wheel, the detective felt a vast contentment. It was so unfamiliar a feeling, so foreign, that he hardly even felt like himself—which wasn't a bad thing by any means.

"You don't know torment. This isn't an exercise in imagination. I'm not inviting you to guess what it's like. You do not know. We break agony down into its tiniest component parts, its atoms, its spectral particles. Then we polish each one. We nurture, we grow, we bring to a supple maturity. After, we start to reassemble. And what begins to take shape is an ultimate suffering. It is a monument to affliction and misery and distress. Then we amplify and elaborate. We do that a thousand times. We do it a billion. We create a living, breathing agony, an intricate and endless fortress devoted to the infliction of pain. When we receive the souls, it is here that we take them, and here that they stay, without reprieve."

Joaquim was humming. It wasn't the start of some hysterical reaction. He was piecing together a lazy tune, some pop ditty from years and years ago, maybe a song he'd shared with Angelica when they were still just boyfriend and girlfriend, not husband and wife.

He eased the Pontiac up toward the crossroads, slowed, stopped. He cut the engine and stepped out with the keys in hand. Gu'ueyun got out the passenger door. The air was cooler than it had been at midnight. He saw a couple of the extinguished tallow candles littering the nearby scrub.

"I don't know how this works," he said, hearing the pleasing steadiness of his voice. The calm and satisfaction didn't leave him. "I don't know if…you take my soul now, or if you wait until I expire naturally, then collect it."

Gu'ueyun moved with a little gingerness. He must have picked up some injuries in that fight. Shreds of his opponent—the wayward demon who had broken the code and helped The Sculptor with his *paltry* crimes—were visible, stuck among his teeth.

"Did you hear what I said in the car?" asked the demon.

"I did."

The night's chill blew softly. Joaquim was no longer sweating. He felt clean, refreshed. He was ready for whatever came next.

Or maybe he wasn't…

"This has been an embarrassment." The low, demonic voice sounded cautious. "My…associate… His violation was a serious one. It might well call the attention of those above in our hierarchy. Or it might have, if I hadn't handled the situation tonight. You helped. I owe you. I won't take your soul. Keep it, abuse it, do what you like."

Abito's eyes blinked, not rapidly or spastically, but he couldn't stop.

Blink blink blink blink.

Gu'ueyun turned and limped, tail twitching weakly, toward that place where earlier the rent had opened. It was swelling wide again, this time without any hoodoo bustle on Abito's part.

When the demon got near the portal, he glanced back, but it wasn't to look at Abito. The hellish creature was eyeing the car, admiration stark on that hideous face.

Detective Joaquim Abito slung the keys to Gu'ueyun, leaving it to the demon to figure out how to take the cobalt blue, cherry GTO back to Hell with him.

Abito turned and started back down the graveled road, marching toward home.

ABOUT THE AUTHOR
ERIC DEL CARLO

Eric Del Carlo has written numerous tales of fiction that attempt to straddle the genres of dark horror and science fiction. Del Carlo's work has appeared in a variety of markets.

Del Carlo's short fiction has appeared in *Asimov's Science Fiction, Strange Horizons, Shimmer* and many other venues. His novels include the Wartorn sword and sorcery series, co-written with Robert Asprin, and the solo novels *Nightbodies* from Ravenous Romance and *The Bleed* from Loose Id.

Del Carlo has worked on a number of collaborative novels, including *Elyria's Ecstasy* from Ellora's Cave with author Amber Jayne and an urban fantasy novel titled *The Golden Gate is Empty* that he co-wrote with his father, Vic Del Carlo. *The Golden Gate Is Empty* is a powerful tale of loss and redemption that explores the deep human emotions involved.

Del Carlo's "We Are Hale, We Are Whole" will be published in the upcoming *Ominous Realities: Collected Works of Dark Speculative Fiction* from Grey Matter Press.

COPYRIGHT DECLARATIONS

MORE FROM GREY MATTER PRESS

A COLLECTION OF MODERN HORROR

DARK

VISIONS 1

VOLUME ONE

EDITED BY

ANTHONY RIVERA AND SHARON LAWSON

DARK VISIONS
A Collection of Modern Horror - Volume One

Somewhere just beyond the veil of human perception lies a darkened plane where very evil things reside. Weaving their horrifying visions, they pull the strings on our lives and lure us into a comfortable reality. But it's a web of lies...

This book is their instruction manual. And it's only the beginning...

DARK VISIONS: A COLLECTION OF MODERN HORROR - Volume One includes thirteen disturbing tales of dread from some of the most visionary minds writing horror, SciFi and speculative fiction today.

DARK VISIONS: A COLLECTION OF MODERN HORROR - Volume One uncovers the truth behind our own misguided concepts of reality.

FEATURING:

Jonathan Maberry

Jay Caselberg

Jeff Hemenway

Sarah L. Johnson

Ray Garton

Jason S. Ridler

Milo James Fowler

Jonathan Balog

Brian Fatah Steele

Sean Logan

John F.D. Taff

Charles Austin Muir

David A. Riley

DARKVISIONSANTHOLOGY.com

 GREY MATTER PRESS

greymatterpress.com

A COLLECTION OF MODERN HORROR

DARK
VISIONS 2
VOLUME TWO

EDITED BY
ANTHONY RIVERA AND SHARON LAWSON

DARK VISIONS
A Collection of Modern Horror - Volume Two

DARK VISIONS: A COLLECTION OF MODERN HORROR - Volume Two begins where the the first one ended.

DARK VISIONS Volume Two continues the terrifying psychological journey with an all-new selection of exceptional tales of darkness written by some of the most talented authors working in the fields of horror, speculative fiction and fantasy today.

Unable to contain all the visions of dread and mayhem to a single volume, *DARK VISIONS - Volume Two* will be available from your favorite booksellers in the FALL of 2013 in both paperback and digital formats.

Prepare to continue the ride with *DARK VISIONS: A COLLECTION OF MODERN HORROR - Volume Two...*

FEATURING:

David Blixt	David Murphy
John C. Foster	Chad McKee
J.C. Hemphill	C.M. Saunders
Jane Brooks	J. Daniel Stone
Peter Whitley	David Siddall
Edward Morris	Rhesa Sealy
Trent Zelazny	Kenneth Whitfield
Carol Holland March	A.A. Garrison

DARKVISIONSANTHOLOGY.com

GREY MATTER PRESS

greymatterpress.com

Made in the USA
Middletown, DE
20 June 2016